CLOSING TIME

CLOSING TIME

Bethan White

Samantha Evergreen

Nikki Turner

Ashley Laino

Lucrezia Brambillaschi

Maryanne Coleman

www.blkdogpublishing.com

They say a stranger is just someone you haven't met yet.

But chance works in mysterious ways.

Several strangers end up at *The Whistler* on Saturday night, a popular pub in London's vibrant and cosmopolitan Soho district.

These strangers will find, when the clock strikes 22:22, that fate and circumstance has linked and intertwined them in ways they could never have imagined.

Welcome to *The Whistler*, we hope you enjoy your stay.

Thanks for covering tonight, Saturdays are a nightmare so I appreciate it. For the music, just press play on the big black thing in my office when you start your shift.

The songs are decided by head office or something. Turn it down if it does your head in, you probably wont be able to hear it over the punters anyway!

Text me if you need anything

Cheers.

- Semisonic – Closing Time

- Chris Isaac – Wicked Game

- George Ezra – Hold My Girl

- The Lumineers – Stubborn Love

- Laura Marling – Ghosts

- Youth – Daughter

- London Grammar – Strong

- Birdy – Wings

- Bon Iver – re:stacks

- The National – England

- Eagle-Eye Cherry – Save Tonight

- Leonard Cohen – Closing Time

- Sigur Rós – Sæglópur

THE
WHISTLER

Meet Me At The Whistler

Bethan White

Some mornings shouldn't really be allowed to go on to become grown-up days. They should be strangled at birth and thrown aside to make way for a better one. But, until the universe gets this method worked out to everyone's satisfaction, a bad day has to run its course. This day opened its eyes full of hope and enthusiasm, as all days do. But within a blink of an eye, it started to go downhill.

'Where were you last night?'

It wasn't the best way to begin any conversation, but because the sentence had been bouncing around in her head all night, in dreams and waking, it seemed as good a way as any other to Amelia.

'Hmmph?'

Again, possibly not the best way to start, but Ben had been startled awake by his phone ringing and he wasn't at his best.

'Last night. Where were you?'

'Here.'

They were not in the mood for social niceties, he because he was still three parts asleep, she because she was an argument waiting to happen. Outside, the sun was shining and, for all she knew, the birds were singing. But she couldn't hear them through the bells of temper ringing in her head. He slid out of bed and headed for the bathroom.

'You didn't answer your phone. I rang and rang.'

'Hmmph.' There was a pause. 'Ah. Ten missed calls. I see that now. I was out of battery. I plugged it in in the kitchen and didn't hear it.'

'And yet, it's by your bed now.'

'How do you know?' He sounded more awake now and more annoyed. 'Have you got the place bugged?'

'No. I just know that you don't sound that sleepy by the time you have got down as far as the kitchen.'

'I don't sound that sleepy in the kitchen when someone's here …'

'Someone?'

'… you're here, because I have woken up properly in bed, if you know what I mean.' There was a significant pause, which she deliberately didn't fill. 'Okay.' He was glad she was there and he was here; when she had one on her, she would argue with the mirror. 'But when I am on my own, when *you* are not here, then I don't usually wake up until I've had a coffee. And I haven't had a coffee yet. I have just picked up the phone for the first time since I plugged it in and forgot it last night.'

She breathed in sharply through her nose and let the breath out noisily. 'It doesn't sound as if you're in the kitchen.'

'Darling, I'm not having this conversation with you. I'm sorry I missed your calls. What did you want?'

'I was going to ask if you wanted to come over.'

'That would have been nice. Shame I missed you.'

She looked at the phone as if it was his face. She was not convinced.

'Darling? Are you there? I said …'

'I heard. What I didn't hear was any regret.'

He sighed. She was beautiful. She was clever. She was … bloody annoying. 'Shall we ring off, let me get some coffee and then do a FaceTime? Perhaps you need to see my face.'

'Let's FaceTime now.' Aha – she'd got him now. She'd see if he was in the kitchen. Or even in his own house. That was by no means a given.

'Look, I need a shit and a shave. I'll call you back in fifteen. Okay?'

'Okay. And that's too much information, by the way.'

He snorted down his nose, in what might have been a laugh. 'Fifteen.' And the line went dead.

She hated herself when she got like this, but she had become totally worked up the night before when she couldn't get through. She started with imagining him dead at the side of the road, his horribly mangled car halfway up a tree. Then she imagined him out with the boys, getting shit-faced in a bar. Then, back to the mangled car. Then she began to picture him in bed with a faceless someone. She couldn't even decide what sex that someone was, as if it really mattered. She had eventually drifted off into an uneasy sleep, filled with dreams of frightening intensity, where blood, gore and waves of desire chased each other all night long. She had woken with a dry mouth and a knot of fear and anger in the pit of her stomach that only a phone call could begin to assuage.

The tousled head appeared from under the covers, where its owner had been trying to block out the call.

'Does she do this a lot?'

'Mothers, eh? I'm still her little boy. She's a bit of an early riser.' He was pushing his feet into slippers and running his fingers through his hair. He ran critical fingers over his chin. He really did need a shave and he had better do that. The shit could wait. 'I'm off for the shave. Do you want to put some coffee on, Chris? That would be good.'

'And then? Make myself scarce, I suppose. I don't think I would be the background you'd want on a call. Mothers can get funny about half dressed women in their son's kitchen of a morning.'

He leaned over the bed and kissed her, the way he knew she liked it. He reached under the covers and she liked it more, rolling onto her back and purring with pleasure. She wasn't as beautiful as Amelia, or as clever, but God – the woman went like a train. After a moment or so, he pulled away.

'Shave.' He pointed to his chest. 'Coffee.' He pointed at her and left the room.

She groaned and rolled over. Sometimes, she wondered why she bothered. Yes, Ben was good-looking but she often didn't like him much. She had a lot to lose in all this; she was *married*, for heaven's sake. And, more complicated still, she had a wife who would be devastated that she was seeing a man. She tried to imagine how the conversation would go and couldn't get beyond the first few words. But ... she swung her legs over the edge of the bed and forced herself upright. But ... this was worth everything. She wasn't sure what chemistry was all about, when it got down to the nitty-gritty of neurons and enzymes, but they had it, in spades. She shrugged on his dressing gown and went downstairs to the kitchen. She put the coffee on and dragged her way back upstairs, dropping the dressing gown on the landing as she went. He had once told her it was her habit of wandering around naked that he loved about her.

He came out of the bathroom and almost cannoned into her as she stood there, lazily scratching her thigh. He bit his lip and reached out, then changed his mind. 'Naughty,' he muttered. 'I'll see you soon. But ...' he glanced at his watch, 'I have to get to work, so we don't have long.'

She leaned forward. 'We don't need long,' she murmured in his ear. 'Now, run down to get your FaceTime, dear. The coffee's on the boil.' She walked into the bedroom and looked over her shoulder. 'As am I.' And she shut the door in his face.

He got to the kitchen just as his phone chirruped, to let him know she was on the line. He flicked the icon sideways and there she was, dressed and made up, hair just so. If she had had a sleepless night, he wasn't going to find out from a FaceTime call.

'Oh.'

'Oh?' His hackles were already rising. He wondered why he bothered, when he had a nice hot woman upstairs, a woman who wouldn't make demands on him like this one did.

'Nothing. Just oh. You managed to work the phone.' She smiled, but it was clearly an effort.

'I think you meant, oh, you really are at home in your own kitchen.' He poured a coffee ostentatiously and sat down at the table.

'Of course I didn't. Look … Ben. I'm sorry. I just got a bit anxious. I …'

He rolled his eyes. 'You didn't ring the police again, did you? Only, last time …'

'No.' She shook her head and the picture blurred. 'No. I remember what you said. It must have been embarrassing … I wouldn't do that again.'

Too damned right it had been embarrassing. He had been upstairs with … actually, he didn't ever get her name, nice woman … and the police had almost beaten his door down. He had told Amelia he was on a Zoom meeting with the US.

'I just … my imagination took over. I'm sorry. I worry when you don't answer.' She looked down and if he had been nearer he knew he would have taken her in his arms and they would be back to square one. Okay for a bit, then back to the same old routine. He had decided more years ago than he cared to remember, that he was simply not a one-woman man. And Amelia was clearly a one-man woman. He just needed it to stop being him.

'Look, Melia, we need to talk.'

'We are talking.'

'I mean *talk*. It's not getting us anywhere, this. What

say we meet up tonight, have a chat, see where we need to go from here.'

She looked up and yes, sure enough, her eyes were filled with tears. 'That sounds serious.'

He smiled at her and her heart turned over. 'It is serious. We need to sort this out once and for all. We'll find a way.'

She brushed away a tear, to the serious detriment of her eye makeup. She forced a smile and he reached out a finger to the screen. She loved it when he did that. 'I …'

'Hush, now. Let's not let the imagination run away with us. Shall we say …? '

'Let's meet where we first met.'

Now, this was awkward. Wherever was that?

'It will be so romantic.'

'Ummm … okay. Let's do that. We don't have to invite everyone else, though, do we?' He hoped that might lay some clues.

'Don't be silly. How could we? We didn't know anyone else there. Let's face it, Ben. You picked me up in a bar. We can't make that sound any better than it was. You didn't ask me my name until the next morning.' Her laugh was hollow.

'I'd drawn a bit of a veil,' he said, sounding as contrite as he could manage. 'I don't do that every day, that's for sure. Perhaps we need to meet somewhere else. Somewhere that *is* romantic.'

'No. The Whistler is fine. But let's have a table this time, shall we? Not just prop up the bar.'

He tried not to let the relief show. The only problem with the Whistler was that it was one of his prime hunting grounds. He would almost certainly get at the very least a quizzical look from the barman. He had recently found out they had a running book behind the bar to see how long it took him from first word to walking out with a woman and the nearest every night got the pot. 'That sounds great. Oh …'

'Oh?' Her eyes were no longer tear-filled but as hard as diamonds.

'I have a meeting.' And the irony was, he really had.

'It's with that office in Japan. Do you remember? You met that guy that time?'

She did indeed remember a Japanese businessman, in the sharpest suit she had ever seen, whose manners, while perfect, were overlaid with such a speculative stare she had spent the evening on tenterhooks in case he suddenly pounced. 'Yes. I remember him.'

'Well, I have a Zoom with him at nine. Shouldn't take too long. It'll be late at the Whistler, but we can come back here afterwards.' He heard the words leave his mouth and he could have cut out his tongue. He didn't intend there to *be* an afterwards.

Her smile was ear to ear. 'That sounds like fun. Umm … do I still have any clean clothes at yours?'

'Er … pretty sure yes.' The last thing he wanted her to do was turn up with a sodding suitcase.

'Great. I can travel light, then. See you at … what shall we say?'

'Any time after ten.'

'See you then. Oh, and Ben?'

'Yes.' He hardly bothered to hide his sigh.

'Love you.'

To his relief, she rang off before he had to answer. He had used the L word, sure he had. But never to mean it. And somehow, he knew with Amelia, he had to mean it. He gave himself a shake and looked down at his lap. He smiled and made for the stairs. He just had time for one more quick one before he had to leave for the office.

'Where were you last night?'

'Darling. We don't do this, do we?'

'I don't know. Don't we?' The woman's voice was cold, but she had clearly been crying. She swallowed awkwardly to clear the tears and coughed.

'I told you. Late meeting. I stayed over with one of the girls from the office.'

'Who?'

'No one you know. She's new.'

The silence cut the air like a knife.

'New? You didn't mention you had anyone new.'

'Well, not new, perhaps. She's a temp.'

'Is she there now?' The voice had just a slight edge of hysteria to it.

'No. She's going to another job today and has to start early. In fact, I have to start soon. She lives a goodish way from the office and I'm not sure I can find the station. I'll need to use my GPS and you know how unreliable that can be.'

'I never have any problem.'

'That's true, my love. But that's because you are a technological wizard and I am an idiot. I'll see you tonight.'

'No, you won't.'

'What?'

'God, hon, don't shout. I'm not leaving or anything. I just mean that I have that meeting, you know, the late one with that Japanese dick. I need to be there to make sure that Mr Thicko manages the Zoom. Otherwise he'll sit there looking at a blank screen all night just waiting for the magic to begin. What say we … oh, bugger it. Let's go out for a drink, like the old days. I'll see you in the Whistler about ten or shortly thereafter. Is that cool?'

'That sounds great. I'll see you there.' She rang off and hugged herself with excitement. With luck, that meant she could grab at least an evening with Ben, if not the whole night. The nights were best, when he pressed himself against her in the dark and they wrestled silently, like strangers meeting in a secret place no one but they knew. She heard his feet on the stairs and threw her phone onto the pile of her discarded clothes from the night before. She rolled on her back and stretched her arms above her head. Thank goodness her wife had such a total arse for a boss. It gave her opportunities she never knew she wanted, but now, couldn't do without.

'Where were you last night?'

Amelia looked down at her friend as she sat riffling through a pile of files.

'Out for a bit, then home.'

'Only, I gave you a call and your voicemail was on.

That's not like you.'

'You didn't ring Bella, did you? Only, she was a bit grumpy with me for going for a drink after work. But she works so late so often, I just didn't think she'd be home.'

'No, I didn't. I was trying to get hold of ...' Amelia wasn't sure why, but she never used Ben's name at work. She liked to be friends with all her staff, it was almost part of her business plan, but sharing that bit was a step too far. '... my boyfriend, but he wasn't answering, so I just thought we might ... well, go out for a drink. You didn't say.'

'Didn't say what?' Tina slid a file into place, ostentatiously. It was okay for the boss to stand gassing all morning, not so much for the grunts. And this wasn't a conversation that was going to end well, if she didn't take a great deal of care.

'That you were going out for a drink.'

'Didn't think I was until I was halfway to the station. And then I just thought "bugger it" and popped into a bar.' She slid in another file and didn't look up.

'I wish I were more like you,' Amelia said. Without looking up, her secretary thought, 'you have no idea'. 'Spontaneous. I never do anything without thinking it over twenty times. I mean ... look at you and Bella. None of us had any idea.'

'Well ... it just seemed right.'

'I mean, we didn't know you were ... you were ...'

Dear God, the woman thought. She can't even say it.

'Well, as I think I explained at the time, I am not actually gay. I am pansexual, which means I am attracted to the person, not their gender.'

Amelia's eyes clouded over. 'Yes, you did say ... But *Bella* is gay, right?'

'She is indeed.'

'Doesn't she ... well, doesn't she *mind*? That you might fancy men?'

'I don't think it occurs to her, actually. But why are we having this conversation at all when I have a pile of filing a mile high?' Tina smiled to take the sting out, but this really was very annoying.

Amelia looked down at the littered desk. In her world, filing was something that happened to other people. 'I didn't even realise we had paper still.'

'Well, yes, we do. And here it is. So …'

'Why do we have paper?'

It struck Tina afresh that Amelia wasn't so much obsessed with her boyfriend and everyone's private life as obsessed with obsessions. Whatever was uppermost in her mind was all her mind contained. And yet, she had developed a very nice niche clothing business which seemed to be going from strength to strength. Perhaps obsession was the key. Bella was obsessed with her and she had a top job as a PA to one of the biggest names in the City. Ben was obsessed with sex, to a degree which most people would call unhealthy, but which Tina just called very, very nice indeed. Amelia was just obsessed, simple as that. And then there was Tina. She wasn't obsessed with anything. She went along with other people's obsessions and so far, they had served her very well. Whenever she crossed Ben's path, she got what they both wanted and when she didn't want it, she stayed away; anyway, she knew he wasn't for keeps. He even called her by the start of her name, not the end like everyone else, having it misheard it in the noise of the Whistler. She lived with her wife in a very smart apartment in a district she had only dreamed of before her marriage. And she worked for Amelia, doing not very much for a more than reasonable sum of money. She looked up at her and smiled again. If she knew what she was thinking … well, may she never know.

'I think it's because you said at the last meeting that we needed physical copies in case of … I don't know. A zombie apocalypse?' Humour was often the way to deflect Amelia. It made her think that you were her friend.

'I suppose we *should* have paper. Oh, dear, it's hard … Do you mind filing?'

'Not at all.' Tina didn't think that this was the moment to say that without filing, she would hardly have a thing to do.

'As long as you don't mind. Where was I before I started obsessing about paper?'

Tina was glad that she was able to laugh out loud in

this office. Friends of hers in other places had been sacked for less. 'You asked where I was last night. And other stuff, but that's where it all began.'

'Oh, yes, right. Well, I'm out tonight, but not until later. Do you want to grab a drink after work?'

'I don't see why not. I'm seeing Bella later as well. Why … before I make an arrangement, I have a call to make. I'll drop you a text.'

'Fine. We could have supper, perhaps, if you're going to be very late seeing Bella.'

'Sounds like a good plan. I'll let you know.' Tina had already got her phone in her hand and sent a message to the number only she knew.

'3 B4 10. U? C.'

In an office not far away as the crow flew, a phone pinged.

'Get that for me, Harry?'

Bella didn't mind that Ben called her by a name none of her friends and family would dream of using. It was just convoluted enough to make him feel clever and if it was a veiled insult from a dyed-in-the-wool homophobe, well, she could take that too. She only ever called him Sir to his face, all kinds of things at home, but never by his name. She didn't see why she should give the arrogant dickhead the pleasure. He was pretty sure he could 'turn' her, as she had heard him braying to his drinking buddies on many an occasion when he was having 'meetings' late into the evening. She didn't mind. Her back was broad and the overtime was even more generous than the salary it went with.

She glanced over. 'It appears to be some bizarre code, Sir.'

He looked over her shoulder and breathed in her scent. It was the same one that Chris used and he felt a little stir. That woman had something special, that was for sure. 'I get the B4 and 10. What in heaven's name does the 3 stand for?'

Bella smiled. The man was a moron. 'I believe it means "free", Sir.'

He mouthed the words, putting them together. 'Oh. I

see. Just reply "No Harry", there's a pet.'

Dutifully, she tapped in the two letters and 'send'. 'Bit terse, Sir, perhaps?' she said.

'Not really. I have just spent the last twelve hours more or less making her scream for mercy, so I doubt she'll take offence.'

Behind his back, Bella screwed up her nose in distaste. Really, what an arse this man was. When she got home, she'd enjoy telling Tina all about it. C? That was a new one; she wondered how long she would last.

Tina spent the morning in the filing room in the basement. Most of the time was spent chatting with the caretaker. He was a great guy, probably fortyish, with so many problems at home that he could make anyone feel grateful, no matter how hard their life might seem. His wife was pregnant again but then, so was his daughter. His mother had just moved in and the other kids were kicking off about having to share a room when Grandma had one to herself.

'Well, I said to them, kids, I said. If any of you want to share with your grandmother, knock yourselves out. Just remember, she farts like a rhino and snores like a Harley. So, up to you.'

Tina laughed and slid the final file into place.

'Does she?'

'Does she what?'

'Fart and snore?'

'I dunno. She's me mother, how would I know that, you weirdo. But I expect so. I know the missus always throws the window open of a morning. She'll have to go when the babies're here.'

'God, Joe, where do you put all these people?'

He shrugged, but smiled. 'I dunno. Sometimes, I forget how many there are. I know we're gonna mislay one of the little 'uns one a these days and we won't notice for weeks.'

Tina knew that wasn't true. It was clear that Joe adored them all. Including his farting mother. Suddenly, she felt a rush in her stomach, a need to tell him … to tell someone … about Ben. She needed to say his name out loud, like a lovesick teenager. 'Joe. Can I ask you something? Well, tell you, really.'

'Course you can, love. Not that I put meself up as a expert.'

'Well, you've seen life, that's clear. It's just that …' Her phone pinged. 'Excuse me a minute.' She rummaged in her pocket and pulled out her phone. No. She blinked. Was that it? The last time she had texted him – though, admittedly, not at work – he had sent her a picture so explicit she had almost cried out. Unfortunate, when watching *Gogglebox* with the missus. She scrolled. No other messages. What a pig!

'So, what's up, Tina?' Joe was a bit intrigued now, especially when she had that expression on her face. 'Don't tell me you're up the spout?'

She shook her head, white to the lips. What an *arse*!

'The missus? The missus is up the spout? You're *both* up the spout?'

Still no answer.

'Tina, you okay? You look terrible, mate.'

She shook her head and looked at him. 'Yes. Umm. Yes, I'm fine.'

'So … whaddya want to tell me?'

'What? Oh, no, nothing. It'll keep.' And she turned on her heel and clattered up the stairs back into the office. She poked her head around Amelia's door. 'Good for supper, if you're still up for it.'

Amelia put up her thumb. It would be good to have some girl talk for a change. She seemed to survive on silence or trying to keep Ben satisfied, which seemed to become less and less possible every day. Never mind. He was going to ask her to move in with him, of that she was certain. He had been so cagey. She shouldn't have put the phone down so quickly after she said she loved him. He probably had felt a bit of a fool, saying it to thin air. She smiled to herself. She'd make it up to him, just see if she didn't.

'So,' Amelia was picking at her quinoa salad. Why she hadn't opted for the cheeseburger she wasn't quite sure. Except that onions always repeated on her and the last thing she wanted to do was to belch a nice stomach full of onion in Ben's face when they got home. 'How is Bella?'

'She's fine. Her boss is a bit of an arse, but that isn't new. The salary is fantastic and she gets to travel quite a bit. Now we're married, I can go on one trip a year. Spousal benefits.' Tina had chosen the cheeseburger and bit into it with relish.

'Wow. That really is some benefit. What perks do I give you guys?'

Tina laughed. 'I think we get half price on the food at the Christmas do.'

Amelia lifted an eyebrow. 'Really? Half price? Now that's what I *call* a deal! Where's the trip likely to be to?'

'Last year, she went to Bali with him. But it might not be there this time. It could be Bognor.'

'What business is he in?'

Tina shrugged. 'Do you know, I have no idea. Buying? Selling? I really don't have a clue. He gets a good bargain with Bella, actually. She's his wing-woman for everything IT as well as being his PA.'

'Lots of initials,' Amelia laughed and inadvertently ate something that tasted like the bottom of a compost heap. She pulled a face. 'What in God's name was that?'

Tina looked closely at her plate. 'God, I have no idea. Why do you eat that muck?' She took another bite of her cheeseburger and wiped the ketchup off her cheek.

'Good question. B ... my boyfriend is a bit funny about what I eat. He doesn't like the smell of onions, stuff like that. So, when we're spending the night together ...'

Tina winked and raised her glass.

'... I stay off onions, obviously, but also things like tuna. Beans. Things that ... repeat.'

Tina laughed and held up her finger while she swallowed her burger mouthful. 'Let me tell you what Joe said this morning. It was priceless.' It was easier to do that than to accidentally say 'well, actually, the chap I am seeing, who makes me scream like a banshee and can keep going all night, also hates onions' – because that was going to be a hard one to explain away. As slips of the tongue went, it wasn't that short.

She told the story, much embellished and with hand gestures until Amelia was laughing so hard she even ate quinoa. Suddenly, she looked at her watch. 'Oh, Tina,' she said, draining her glass, 'I must dash. I'm meeting …'

'Of course.' Tina pushed back her chair. 'So am I. Well, not your chap, of course. Bella. She was helping with a Zoom meeting.'

'It never fails to amaze me,' Amelia said, waving her credit card at the waitress, 'No, really, Tina, I'll get this. Call it a staff benefit. It never fails to amaze me, these men in these high powered positions, who can hardly manage FaceTime. You'd think they'd at least try to learn, wouldn't you?'

Again, Tina bit her lip. One of these days, she knew, she was going to slip up. It was coming to the point where she was going to have to give Ben up or just tell Bella she was playing away from home and she could take it or leave it. It was just getting too hard.

They made their way to the door and stepped outside.

'Oh,' Tina said, surprised. 'It's been raining.'

Amelia looked up at the sky. 'It doesn't look as if it's going to come on again,' she said. 'And it wasn't much, by the look of the road. Look, no puddles to speak of.'

'I hope not,' Tina said. 'This coat isn't even shower-proof. Which way are you going?'

Amelia pointed to her left. 'Down here. I must admit, I was a bit naughty. I have had my suspicions that … well, that we may be drifting apart. So I suggested we meet where we met first and he knew where that was.' She looked down and smiled. 'I think … well, I think he might be asking me something quite important tonight.'

'Proposing? Wow!' Tina was surprised. She had never got the impression that the Mystery Man as they called him in the office was all that serious. He certainly seemed to be away a lot.

'Well, don't quote me on that,' Amelia hedged. 'But to move in, yes, I think that. He said we needed to have a serious chat.'

Tina bit back the words which almost left her mouth. Looking at Amelia, beautiful, rich, successful, she could well imagine that being dumped was not something she had experienced that often, if at all. And perhaps, she gave herself a metaphorical slap on the wrist, she wasn't going to now. But she would be prepared for tears in the office in the morning.

They turned down a side road and kept chatting companionably. A sudden commotion in front of them made them step to one side. A group of men were silhouetted against the light spilling from a kebab shop. For a moment, it was hard to see why they looked so odd then, suddenly, they were upon them and it was clear. The costumes, home-made, were more or less successful but the general gist was that these men, mostly sporting beer bellies and fat backsides, were the Power Rangers. The one in pink hadn't been that bothered at first that when he picked the name 'Shelby' out of the hat, but he was bothered now and was by far the drunkest of the group. He draped himself over Amelia and slurred something in her ear. She pushed him off.

'Certainly not,' she shrieked. 'I don't care what you have in your tights! You're drunk, all of you. You're disgusting.'

The one in purple lurched forward, brandishing a moulting kebab. 'We're drunk, possibly,' he said. 'But …' he closed his eyes and swayed for a while before suddenly coming to. '… we're not dishgusting. No. Getting married, me. But not dishgusting.' He seemed to have lost the power of forward locomotion until one of the men, dressed in blue and actually quite fetching, Tina thought, moved them all forward.

'Designated driver,' he said with a smile as he passed. 'Come on, you lot. Leave the ladies alone. Mush. Come on. Off we go.'

The side road seemed rather quiet when they had gone. Amelia checked her coat for shed kebab.

'He was rather dishy, the one in blue lycra,' Tina said, for something to say.

Amelia looked at her. 'I keep forgetting …' she said.

'It's nothing,' Tina said. 'Do you know the sexual preferences of all your staff? And does it matter if you do or don't? I wish I'd never said anything.'

'You can't hide the fact you're married,' Amelia said.

'Why not? Jack's married. Did you know?'

Amelia stopped dead. 'Jack's *married*? When did that happen?'

Tina shrugged. 'Six months. Eight. I don't know. They went on holiday and when they came back – married.'

'Well.' Amelia blew out her cheeks. 'I had no idea.'

'Well, that's what I mean. We don't know what your boyfriend's called, do we? We don't know how many children Joe has ... although to be fair, I don't think he's sure himself.'

'Ben,' Amelia said, suddenly.

'Pardon?'

'Ben. My boyfriend's name is Ben.'

'Gosh, well ...'

'Gosh, well, what?'

Tina could hardly say that she was seeing someone with just that name. 'Gosh, well, thanks for sharing.'

'Time I did. Now you tell me something.'

'Nothing to tell.'

'Everyone has something.' Amelia stopped and pulled on Tina's arm. 'Stop a minute. Pretend you're looking in this window. I haven't brought you out of your way, have I? Just thought.'

'No, no. You're fine. But why ...?'

'That woman down there. Drunk as a skunk. We'll wait until she's gone.'

'Bella!' Ben pressed keys at random. 'Bella! What's happening here?'

Bella pushed back her chair and sighed. Surely, surely even he couldn't mess up a Zoom invitation. Read. Click. Done.

'What seems to be the problem?' She leaned over him and he was engulfed in Chris's perfume again. He inhaled and then tried to bring himself back to meeting mode.

'No one seems to be there. Look.' He stabbed random-ly at the keyboard and pointed at the screen, which was blank. Bella wondered again how he managed to make a liv-ing at a level which would make most people blink.

She pressed some keys with practiced fingers and suddenly the screen was alight with squares, each containing a rather disgruntled-looking Japanese businessman, including the one she had met. 'There you are,' she murmured in his ear, making sure she kept out of camera-shot. He was an idiot, but she didn't want the world to know; she liked this lifestyle and if she had to make him look intelligent to keep it, so be it.

'Thanks,' he said out of the corner of his mouth, before going into total business mode. He didn't function quite so well when he couldn't press the flesh, but he was getting better. She stood behind the monitor so as to be invisible. She clicked her fingers and he looked up briefly. She mimed tapping keys and then slapped her own hand, making a throat-cutting motion with one finger. Then, to be doubly clear, she shook her head. He waved at her to show he understood. She sighed again and went to wait in the outer office. He was sometimes a bit of a fiddler and had cut off many a meeting in its prime, over the years.

She sat at her desk and read. She never ended a day with work outstanding and she was just here to back him up, the techno-idiot to beat them all. She wasn't like the other secretaries. She didn't play stupid games involving shooting balls or crushing candy. She had never seen the point. She didn't listen to music. It all sounded the same to her. She read Golden Age crime and could spot a pastiche at a distance of a thousand paces. Her reviews had come to be feared the length and breadth of Amazon. This one was real, sure enough. A George Bellairs, as transparent as they came, but engagingly written, even if she did know by page nine that the vicar did it. The Japanese voices and the staccato translations swept over her and went on their way, disregarded.

'Bella!'

She pushed her chair back and didn't bother with the sigh.

'Yes, Sir?'

'How do I hang up, again?'

'No need. The connection has closed and we're all good. Do you want to transcribe your notes now, or leave it until the morning?'

He knew how she hated leaving things and toyed with waiting, just to wind her up. But on the other hand — he glanced at his watch — he didn't want to be early for meeting Amelia. He needed to walk up to her table, not the other way about. That way, he could just lean over, tell her it wasn't her, it was him. No, wait, that wasn't going to work. It *was* her. She was unreasonable, jealous and frigid. Yes, that ought to do it. He'd dress it up a bit, of course. So he had some time to kill.

'Let's do it now. I don't need to set off for ...' he looked at his watch, '... another fifteen, I shouldn't think. What about you?'

She looked at him, dubiously. Since when had he ever cared about her?

'I need to do about the same,' she said. 'I'm meeting Tina in the Whistler any time after ten. I ...' she looked down.

'You?' He wasn't in the slightest bit interested, but he was a people person and knew how to keep a conversation going when only five per cent of his brain was on board.

'Well,' she didn't stop to think that this probably wasn't what he wanted to do. She had been chewing over all day and needed to get it out. 'I think Tina may have met someone else.'

His head came up. So, everything was not all roses in Lesbianland? That was just the kind of thing he liked to hear. He pushed his notes aside. 'Do you want to talk about it?' He *did* hope she did!

'No. No, I don't think so. Let's get these notes transcribed. While it's all fresh in your mind. I've already got the list of attendees, so we can go from point one.'

Sighing, he pulled his pad over again. She was a hard nut to crack, but crack her he would, if it took forever. The day had been quite stressful, one way and another. The translator had probably been the worst ever — he had almost needed a translator himself. 'Okay. Point one. No, hang on, I must just ...' He pulled out his phone, the non-work one, and scrolled down the messages. There were quite a few, from cursory to downright filthy – he'd check those later. He found the one from Chris and clicked on it. Slowly, using his fore-finger in a way that made Bella want to explode with laughter, he picked out, 'Sorry. Sent no by mistake. I'll be all done by 10.25 latest. See you mine?' He paused for a mo-ment, then added 'xxx'. He smiled up at Bella. If the day had not been very special, at least he knew he was okay for the night. 'Right. Point one.'

'What's she doing?' Amelia didn't like public displays of drunkenness any more than public displays of affection, but this was looking pretty hilarious. The woman currently lurch-ing around in the street was shouting the odds with a passing taxi. She had hailed him and he was about to pull up when he realised how drunk she was. But by this time, she had hold of his door handle and he would have hurt her badly if he had driven off; she was clearly too off her face to manage to let go in time. She had lost a shoe, hadn't she? No, looking closer, she had nude courts on – Amelia grimaced; *so* old hat! – and one of them had lost a heel, giving her a cock-eyed gait. Her blouse was out on one side and her hair was all over the place. It wasn't even that late – Tina checked her phone and it wasn't even ten – but she was properly shit-faced. She shook the cab's door handle but it wouldn't open. Suddenly – so suddenly she almost fell over backwards – she stepped away and swung her arm back and over, landing a perfect strike with a half-eaten kebab in the middle of the wind-screen. An elderly gent on the other side of the road gave vent to a quiet 'Howzat' and then hurried on before the woman realised who had spoken.

The woman continued spinning round with her own momentum. The shoe with no heel was giving her balance problems but she couldn't work out what was causing her unfortunate tendency to lurch to the left. A couple of her friends had followed her out of the kebab shop and, although by no means as pissed as her, were also very much the worse for wear.

Then, suddenly, the sound of approaching Power Rangers grabbed her attention and she bent forward, peering up the street. She rocked back and forth, trying to get them into focus and had still not succeeded when they swept past, taking her and her friends into their orbit like giant planets sucking up space debris. The designated driver, still luscious in blue, smiled apologetically as they went by.

Tina's phone pinged and she glanced down at the screen. She gave a wry smile and put it back in her pocket.

'Something important?' Amelia was nothing if not nosy.

'No. Just a pointless message. That's the trouble with WhatsApp – once you join a group, you can never control it.'

'A group?' Amelia had never been asked to join a group. 'How does that work?'

'Well, you know. Like at work. We have a group so we …' Tina realised she was not going to get anywhere. Amelia was in a group of one. Interests; Ben. Tina looked at her for a minute. It wasn't possible, was it, that …? No. Her Ben wouldn't look twice at a needy creature like Amelia. He was strictly a love 'em and leave 'em kind of guy and would run a mile.

Amelia was shaking her head and Tina smiled and patted her arm.

As ever, Ben kept Bella waiting, while he went into the gents to primp and make sure he was looking his lovely best. He spent more time titivating than any other woman Bella had ever known. One of the things – one of the *many* things, she reminded herself crossly – that she loved about Tina was she could be up and ready to go within minutes. She slipped out her phone from her bag and sent her a quick message. Not using her forefinger and with her mouth hanging open like a goldfish. 'Running a bit late because Mr Thicko is primping in the loo. Get the drinks in – mine's a double! Bxxx'

Ben finally emerged from the gents smelling like a tart's boudoir. Bella tried not to wrinkle her nose. Did that really work on women?

'Are we set?' he said, rubbing his hands together. He looked at his watch. 'Come on, we need to put a bit of a wiggle on or we'll be late.'

Bella looked at him, uncertain how to respond. So, she had made them late, had she? God, how she hated this man.

'Perhaps now the drunks have gone, we can get to the bar?'

Tina's phone gave a ping. She smiled a rueful smile at Amelia and fished again for her phone. She flicked to the message and chuckled.

'Another WhatsApp group?' Amelia's voice could have etched glass.

'No, no, just Bella. Her boss is probably the vainest man in London, if not on earth, so he's in the loo. Primping, Bella says.' And with another chuckle, she put her phone away.

'Well,' Amelia by now was in the mood to fight with herself. 'I prefer a man who takes care of himself, as opposed to …' she looked around and saw no one she could find fault with. 'As opposed to that idiot in blue you seem to fancy so much.'

'For goodness sake, Amelia,' Tina said, still chuckling. 'I don't fancy him! He's just the best of a bad bunch. And I don't expect he dresses like a Power Ranger all the time. He's probably, oh, I don't know, a brain surgeon. A tree surgeon. Who cares?'

'I would have you know,' Amelia said, 'that my Ben washes from head to toe before we … well, you know.' Her high horse was about to gallop away with her.

'Gosh.' There seemed little else to say.

'Gosh, what?'

'Well, gosh, that's not very spontaneous. Has he never rushed in when you open the door, ripped your clothes off and just had you, there and then, in the hall?'

Amelia looked her up and down as if she was pond slime suddenly walking and talking. 'That is *totally* disgusting,' she said. 'It might be *literally* the most disgusting thing I have ever heard.'

Tina shrugged. 'Up to you,' she said. 'Disgusting if you say so, but also a lot of fun.' She smiled and that was her undoing.

'You're *filthy*!' Amelia raged. 'You're *disgusting*! You're *fired!*' And she stormed off back the way they had come.

'Say *what?* You can't fire me for that!'

Amelia spun round and pointed with a finger now completely out of her control. 'Oh? Really? Watch me!' and spun round again. Inevitably, she fell into the gutter and rested there on her hands and knees, sobbing with anger and pain.

Tina ran up to her and helped her to her feet. With gentle fingers, she wiped away her tears, leaving her mascara intact. She held her by the shoulders. 'Now,' she said, as though to a child, not her boss. 'Calm down. You're over excited because of moving in with Ben. But you don't want to turn up looking like that, do you? Now, walk with me, yes, that's right, this way, away from the pub, give yourself time.'

Amelia gave an industrial-size sob and took a deep breath.

'That's it. Now, let's have a look at your knees.'

Obediently, Amelia held out a leg.

'Great. No blood. No bruising. You're fine.'

With Tina's arm around Amelia, they walked slowly down the road, the racking sobs slowly diminishing until, with a final sniff, Amelia said, 'That's fine, Tina. You can let go now. You're not fired.' She looked at her watch, a Rolex bought for its sheer ostentation. 'Oh, God, look at the time. I'm late.'

Tina flicked out her phone. 'Actually, you're on time. Who wants to get there on the dot? You said after ten, didn't you? Well, it's just gone ten past. Plenty of time to let him get a drink and be ready to pop his question.'

Ben always forgot that Bella's legs were shorter than his and he had soon left her in his wake. Actually, that wasn't strictly true – he didn't even stop to consider whether she could keep up. He just set off for his destination and left her in his wake. After a sharp right turn or two, she stopped even bothering and dropped her pace to a saunter. After the rain earlier in the evening, which had spattered on the glass wall of her office while The Thicko was struggling with a Japanese non-translator, it was pleasant to stroll through the quiet streets to meet her wife. She was glad she hadn't thrown her toys out of the pram. If she couldn't trust her, what future did they have? Turning the final right, she saw him disappear into the Whistler. And good riddance, she thought. Good luck to the woman of the week – she'd need it.

Amelia smiled and put her hand up to smooth Tina's cheek. 'I'm sorry,' she said. 'I've bought you out of your way, and now I must dash. I really hate being late.' And, suiting the action to the words, she trotted off back the way they had come and disappeared into the Whistler.

Tina kept her back turned once she had seen her on her way. She had two texts to send. One was simple. It just said. 'No.' Then she paused and sent another to the same number. It said 'Sod Off.' She felt better for that.

Bella slowed a little. She wanted Ben to be tied up with whatever he had planned before she walked in. She didn't want to get involved with that can of worms. She counted slowly under her breath, with one step every three seconds. But even with that strategy, all too soon, she turned into the Whistler.

Still smiling at the thought of how Ben would react, Tina turned and walked slowly down the road towards the Whistler, texting as she went. 'We both need a triple! I'll get them in xxx'

She pressed send and waited while the two ticks appeared. The message was timed at 22.22 as she turned in at the door.

The Blue Power Ranger

It had seemed a bit of a no-brainer at first, that the stag do costumes should be based on the Power Rangers. There had been six of them, so the colours would be simple to dob out (though the pink one caused a bit of controversy) and it seemed very apt that he had drawn Billy, the nerd in blue. Because, it had to be said, he was a bit of a nerd. It was therefore obvious that he would also be the designated driver. He was always the designated driver. And yet he always seemed to end up paying the same when they split the bill. But never mind; as well as being the nerd, he was also the nice one.

As his co-stags lurched down the road, ogling a couple of women on their way, leaving a kebaby hand-print on one of them's arse, he actually was feeling pretty good about his current persona. He knew that his costume was correct in every detail, down to the blue diamonds airbrushed onto his white wellies. The green Power Ranger seemed to be dressed in a pair of pyjamas with the jacket tucked in and the man in blue was disappointed that not everyone had bothered. One of the idiots was in purple. Purple? Where did purple come into it? He just didn't want to be yellow, which was a girl. He sighed. He knew he shouldn't worry about this kind of detail, but he did. He would be a nerd all his life, no question.

The plans for this stag do had, foolishly, been left in the hands of the stag, who couldn't organize his way out of a wet paper bag. His fiancée was just as bad, if not worse – her group of hens was around and about in London somewhere, no doubt throwing up in a gutter and jostling to see who ended up going home with the stripper – as he understood it, he was going to be dressed as a policeman; how very original. The stag, the copped out yellow one who was actually purple, was now so wasted that even if they had bothered to spring for a stripper, he would have had nothing in his armoury to make it worth her while.

The blue Power Ranger did his blue Power Ranger best to keep them in order, but it was like herding cats. Like herding drunken cats. So when one of them did a one-eighty at the end of the road and started heading back the way they had come, he let it happen. At the kebab shop, as they slid and slithered through their own detritus dropped so recently, they somehow managed to snag a trio of drunken women, so much older than them that it wasn't even funny. The blue Power Ranger looked wistfully at the rather prettier of the two women they had already molested, but she seemed to be dealing with her friend who had fallen over and was wailing about something.

He sighed and closed his eyes. How long did you have to stay at a stag do? If he sloped off at ten, would anyone notice? Probably. He promised himself; twenty past, and not a second later.

How To Be An Octopus

Nikki Turner

An octopus can have its leg ripped off and grow a new one. Did you know that? The sea must be a scary place if you need to have a superpower like that. Sometimes I pretend to be an octopus just floating along on the current. Next thing a scary shark eats my arm. I squirt ink into the water to confuse him and escape. Then I pull my arm into my jersey and hug it to my side. Slowly, as my arm regrows, I poke it back into the sleeve. My mum says it is a very strange game, but I like it.

My name is Maya and I'm six years old. I know a lot of interesting facts. Every morning when I wake up, I'm allowed to turn on the TV as long as I watch nature documentaries. Mum says regular TV makes your brain rot. I saw a rotten apple once. It was all mushy and brown juice leaked out of it. I often stare at people on the tube to see if I can spot brown juice leaking out of their ears. Most people watch lots of TV so there must be loads of rotten brains around.

My favourite nature programmes are by Sir David Attaburger. He has a very posh voice and he always makes you feel sad for the animals that are going to die. Sometimes one of them gets away and then I jump up and down on the couch and shout. I don't shout too loud because mum is usually still asleep. She says she's a night owl and I'm an early bird. One of the big boys in our building told us a scary story about a man in a black cloak who turns into a bat at night. Then he flies around sucking people's blood. He sounds like bad news to me. If mum is a night owl, maybe she turns into a bird at night and swoops across London protecting people from the bat man. She's a secret superhero, I think. Once I tried to stay awake to catch her. But it's just like at Christmas. I always try to stay awake so I can catch Father Christmas dropping off my presents. I want to ask him if I can go for a ride in his sleigh with Rudolph's nose lighting up the night. But I always fall asleep too soon.

The programme I'm watching today is not as good as one of Sir David's. My tummy is sore from hunger, so I pull out a chair to fetch a bowl from the cupboard. I have to be very careful; I can only reach the bowls if I go on my tippy toes. Then I put cereal into the bowl and eat it in front of the TV. I take big bites like a hungry lion. None of the Froot Loop animals can escape me!

Finally, Mum shuffles into the room and I bounce over and throw my arms around her. She ruffles my hair. 'Morning, Maya mouse. How did you sleep, baby?'

'I don't know how I slept. I can't see myself when I'm asleep.'

Mum laughs and puts my bowl into the sink. She pours water and takes her happy pills out of the cupboard. I'm not sure why she needs them because I make her laugh all the time. But she says they're just for a bit of extra happiness. My happy pills are Smarties. They're my favourite. If you could lick a rainbow, I bet it would be Smartie flavoured. Mum says all the colours taste the same, but she's wrong. The blue ones definitely taste the best. I save all the blue ones till last and then suck them till they melt. I end up with a bright turquoise tongue. Sometimes, if we're on the bus coming home, I stick it out at people. They must think I'm turning into a Smurf.

Mum leans against the counter holding her coffee. 'So, today's the big day.'

I can't think for a minute what she means and then I remember. I blurt, 'It's job interview day. You're going to get this one, mum.'

She smiles and her dimples wink at me. 'You think so, Maya mouse?'

I puff out my chest. 'I know so. You're the prettiest, cleverest mum in the whole wide world.'

And that's the absolute truth. My mummy is very young and pretty, much younger than other mummies. She says she wanted to be a nurse but then she had me and couldn't stay at school. This made me sad. But when she saw that, she said that having me was the best thing that ever happened to her. So, that's okay then. I'm starting school in a week's time so now mum will have time for a job. It will be her very first one, so she says she's a bit scared. But I know she'll be brilliant!

Mum asks, 'Have you brushed your teeth, baby?'

I press my lips together and nod my head. In the morning I have dragon breath, says mum. I fly around the flat breathing on things and burning them to a crisp. Then I use my magic dragon powers to fix it all before she wakes up. Mum pulls me closer and says, 'Let's smell.'

I try blow out as little air as possible but her nose crinkles. 'Go brush your teeth, please. I can't take a dragon out of the house.'

I brush my teeth and make silly faces at myself in the mirror. Mum comes into the bathroom to brush my hair and I see she's wearing my favourite tracksuit, which means this job interview is a Big Deal. A lot of her clothes are faded and stretched, but this is almost brand new. It's green and made of velvet. Mum says the material is something much cheaper, but I think she's wrong. When we went to watch the Christmas pantomime, the theatre seats were made of velvet. I missed a big part of the show because I liked the feeling of it so much, I couldn't stop stroking it. Mum told me that queens used to wear long, velvet dresses which I think is very silly. They must have swept up the dust everywhere they walked. Although I suppose that kept their castles very clean.

We walk hand in hand downstairs to Mrs. Stein's flat. She's going to look after me while mum's out. But when she opens the door, her nose is bright red and her eyes are all runny. She does a big, dramatic sneeze into her hanky. Mum is always telling me I'm dramatic, but Mrs. Stein couldn't possibly have needed to sneeze that loudly. She's just looking for attention.

'I'm so sorry, love, but I've come down with a dreadful cold. I can't possibly watch Maya this afternoon. I feel like a truck has run over me.'

I inspect her dressing gown with interest, looking for telltale track marks. I look up at mum's face and she's the one who looks like she's been hit by a truck.

'But… but… I've got this interview and all. What'll they think if I just pitch up with my kid? Maya will be ever so quiet and not bother you at all, I promise. Quiet as a mouse, hey Maya?'

I nod my head and put a finger to my lips. Mrs. Stein has another explosion of a sneeze.

'I feel terrible to let you down, love, but I just can't today. I'm sure they'll understand the situation.'

She closes the door almost onto our noses. Mum just stands there for a little bit. Then she says, 'Right then. Come along Maya, off we go baby.'

She is holding my hand very tightly, so that it's almost sore. I give hers a little squeeze and she looks down at me. 'Sorry, was I hurting you?' I shake my head furiously and she smiles. 'Off we go on an adventure, baby. Maybe you'll be my good luck charm today.'

I'm going to be the bestest good luck charm. Like a four-leaf clover and a lucky penny rolled into one.

***

Did you know that starfish can also grow new arms if they lose one? Even better, the arm that falls off can turn into a brand-new starfish. It's a bit weird but also very interesting. Mum told me a story about a whole bunch of starfish that washed up on a beach. They were dying as they lay there out of the sea. When an old man saw a little girl trying to throw them back, he told her not to bother. That there were too many and she wasn't making a difference. She threw another one into the waves and said, 'At least I made a difference for that one.'

If I spoke to an old man like that my mum would tell me not to be cheeky and to respect my elders. But I think starfish girl is very cool. She's an eco-warrior like mum and me. When we got off the tube in Soho and started walking to the interview, we picked up all the plastic lying on the ground and put it in the bin. There were so many straws which made me cross. Straws choke the sea turtles and mum only lets us use paper ones. People can be very selfish, I think. Mr Sea Turtle doesn't have a choice, but we do.

Mum's interview is at a pub called The Whistler where her best friend Carly works. Mum and Carly had babies on almost the same day and have been best friends since then. Carly's daughter Eva is my best friend in the whole, wide world so it all worked out very well for us. While we were in our mum's tummies maybe we already whispered to each other through their bellybuttons. That's why we were friends forever straight away.

Soho is very busy, so I cling onto mum's hand. I don't want to get lost in the crowds. Mum tells me if I ever get lost, I must just go find a policeman. Then I can give him mum's mobile number which I know off by heart. But I've been looking out for one and haven't seen any yet. We did walk past the Smiggle store just now. Eva gave me a Smiggle pencil case for my birthday which is what I always wanted. That's what best friends do; they make your dreams come true. I think if I get lost, I'll go back to that store. The ladies who work there must be very kind and love children. I'm sure they would be happy to help me. Those ladies definitely won't be Bad People. Mum has told me about Bad People who give little girls sweets and steal them from their mummies. I asked why they steal girls, but mum shook her head and wouldn't tell me. I think it's so they can have someone to wash their clothes and clean their floors. If I got stolen, I'd end up like Cinderella, having to do all the work for someone very cross and scary. I hold mum's hand just a tiny bit tighter.

Finally, we're standing outside The Whistler. I've never been here before, but I have been to a pub. Sometimes on a Sunday in summertime, Mum and I catch the train to Sussex. It's where Mum grew up. We go to a pub called The Old Lion and sit in the beer garden to eat fish and chips. My grandparents still live in Sussex, but we don't go to visit them. Mum says they are very old and senile. Which means they won't remember who we are. I'm not so sure about this. Sir David Attaburger is ancient, and he still knows all about animals. Maybe my grandparents watched too much TV and rotted their brains.

We go inside and Aunty Carly rushes over to us. I call her aunty even though we're not related. Mum says the best family is the family you choose for yourself. She gives me a big hug then looks up at mum. 'I thought Mrs. Stein was looking after Maya?'

'She was supposed to, but she's come down with a cold. So, I had to bring her along.'

Carly wipes her hands down her apron, checking over her shoulder. 'Maybe I can ask to take a quick break. Then I can take Maya down the road to…'

Before Carly can finish speaking, a boy with very bad skin interrupts her. 'Carly, is this your friend? The one who's here for the interview?'

Surely, this can't be the manager who's going to interview mum. He looks younger than her. Like he should still be at school.

Carly nods her head. 'Pete, this is Sienna.'

Mum sticks out her hand, but he just looks at her. I don't like his face. His pimples look violent. It's a good word for them because it is a colour and a feeling. Mum says you must never say unkind things about people. But I'm not saying them, I'm thinking them. And I really don't like the expression on his face as he looks at us.

He licks his lips and says, 'Sienna, is it? Well, isn't that posh. Bit of a come down for a posh girl like you, wanting to come work at the Whistler, hey?'

Mum's face turns bright red and she mumbles, 'No, no, not at all. I'm so excited about the interview. I really am…'

The pimply boy interrupts her, 'Didn't exactly dress to impress, did you? And you bought your kid along. That's getting off on the wrong foot, isn't it?'

Mum is hanging her head and she has her arms crossed tightly across her chest. Now it's Carly's face that has turned tomato red. 'Look, Pete, there's no need to talk to her that way. She's a single mum, right. Her babysitter got sick. Cut her a break.'

Pete turns on Carly and snaps, 'Not going to be much use to me when she keeps cancelling shifts because she doesn't have a sitter. I know her type, living it up on the dole. Having kids just to get a council house.'

Mum's head flies up and she almost shouts, 'Don't you ever talk about my daughter like that. Like she's nothing but a meal ticket.'

Pete steps closer to her and as he pushes a finger into her face, I see red. I am a hungry lion. I am a fire breathing dragon. Nobody talks to my mum like that. I launch myself forwards and sink my teeth into Pete's calf. He howls and tries to shake me off. I grind my teeth in even deeper. He's screaming now, 'Get your bloody brat off my leg. I'll kick her if she doesn't bloody let go.'

Mum drops to her knees and whispers, 'Maya, please, you're hurting him. Please, stop.'

Only because Mum asked me too.

'Get out! Take your bloody little demon child and get out!'

Then mum and I are back on the street. Carly has rushed out with us and is whispering to mum frantically. They hug and Carly goes back inside the pub. Mum looks at me, then kneels down next to me right on the pavement. I reckon I'm in big, big trouble now. She takes a tissue out of her bag and wipes my face. Then she smooths the hair back from my forehead and kisses me. She doesn't say another word till we get home.

* * *

Mum has made me a hot chocolate and is letting me watch the Disney channel. We are cuddling on the couch, so I know she's not that cross with me about biting pimply Pete. I don't get treats or TV if I've been naughty. I didn't even get a time-out! When mum's phone rings, she puts it on speaker so I can also hear. Aunty Carly's voice floats into the room.

'Hey, Sienna, I'm just calling to see if you and Maya are okay. Sorry, it's been mad busy all afternoon or I would have called sooner.'

Mum has a strange, twisted little smile on her face. 'So, I take it I didn't get the job then?'

There's a long pause. Mum gives a loud snort and starts to laugh. So does Carly. I join them because it feels good to giggle after this horrible afternoon.

You can hear that Carly is smiling when she speaks again. 'No, I can definitely say you didn't get it. But if it makes you feel better, Pete had to go to the emergency room for a tetanus shot and those hurt like a bit... choo hoo. Whoops, that one almost slipped out of me. Sorry, Maya mouse.'

I know what word Carly was going to say. It's a very, very bad word. Mum says she'll give me a spoon of hot sauce if she ever hears me saying it. I wonder if she would have given one to Carly.

Carly says, 'That's actually why I'm calling. Pete took the rest of the day off and I'm finishing my shift in an hour. Why don't you come back to the pub and have a drink with me? Sam behind the bar is so mad at Pete for how he treated you, he says he'll comp us for the evening. Nothing like some free drinks with your best friend to cheer you up.'

Mum puts her arm around me and pulls me close. 'But what about Maya? Mrs Stein won't have her. Where's Eva tonight?'

'She's with my mum for the weekend.'

Carly's mum lives in Sevenoaks. We visited her once and it was a long ride on the train.

Mum says, 'I don't think I can. The Whistler isn't the best place for a kid on a Saturday night.'

I can hear in her voice how much she really wants to go. I try to talk to mum telepathically. That means talking to someone with your mind, not your mouth. I want her to know that I think The Whistler would be a great place for us tonight.

'Nonsense.' Carly is using her bossy voice. She does that when she thinks she knows what's best for mum. 'We mainly get people stopping for a bite on their way to the theatre shows. This isn't Brixton. We won't stay late, and I'll buy Maya anything she wants for supper. It'll be good for you to get out. Plus, it'll be giving the finger to Pete, big time.'

I don't know what this finger is. Mum read me a book called *The Magic Finger* once, but I don't think that's what Aunty Carly means.

Mum is humming under her breath. I pull on her t-shirt and make big eyes when she looks at me. I am trying to be as cute as possible so that she won't say no.

'Pleeeeeease,' comes Carly's voice over the speaker.

'Pleeeeeease,' I mimic.

Mum throws her hands up into the air. 'Fine, the two of you win. What time shall we meet you there, Carly?'

'I'll be done by 8pm. Fantastic, I'm thrilled you're coming. We'll drink away those sorrows of yours and maybe I can even stretch to a pudding for Maya.'

I start bouncing on the couch and mum gives me a fierce look. She says the couch is not a trampoline. Personally, I think it makes an excellent trampoline. Grown-ups have no imagination.

I run through to the bedroom to change my clothes. If I'm going to the pub at night for the first time, I am going to make sure I look extra fancy. I have a sparkly dress we got in the sales and a pair of red ballet pumps. Everyone is going to gasp when I walk in. I twirl in front of the mirror and practice some poses. Beautiful, just like a princess. Mum is standing in the doorway with her head tipped to one side. 'You look beautiful, Maya.'

I spin to face her and squeal, 'That's just what I was thinking!'

This makes mum laugh a lot which makes my heart give a happy gallop. She puts on jeans and a black t-shirt. She adds black liner around her eyes and when she is done, she looks just like a model in a magazine. When I tell her that she shakes her head and hugs me. 'Now Maya, if the pub gets too rowdy, we're going to come straight home. I don't want you making any fuss about it. We won't be staying late, just a quick drink and bite to eat. Okay?'

I nod my head as fast as I can. It is so exciting to be going out at night with mum that I'll take anything I can get.

I dance the whole way to the station. People keep looking at me and grinning. Knowing all eyes are on me, I dance even harder. When the tube comes, I'm too excited to sit down. Instead, I hang onto the rail and curtsey at everyone who looks at me. I am Her Royal Highness, Maya the First of Wandsworth. I am sometimes a dragon and sometimes a lion. I can grow new arms like an octopus. My mother is Queen Sienna the Night Owl. My father is a mysterious prince under the spell of a wicked witch. I smile and wave my hand at everyone who gets off. They laugh and wave back. Then before you know it, we are back outside The Whistler. I wonder whether there will be a bloodstain on the floor from Pete's leg. I would really like that.

Inside, Aunty Carly waves frantically to us from a corner table. There are two glasses of wine already waiting and a very interesting glass filled with something bright green. I hope it's cream soda, which mum doesn't usually let me have. Carly jumps up to hug us both and whispers in my ear, 'Thought it was a cream soda kind of day.'

I give her a wink which I only learned how to do this last week. Mum says I'm not winking, just scrunching up both my eyes. But Carly winks back and I feel a little glow of triumph.

We sit down and mum hands me a menu. This is a very important decision, so I take my time. My first meal out in a pub at night, it needs to be something special. Something I will remember for the rest of my life. I order a hamburger with mushroom sauce and cheesy fries. Burgers in restaurants are not like the ones from McDonald's. Mum never lets us get takeaway from there, because she says the meat is all the mashed-up bits of cow that nobody else wants to eat. That is very gross and I'm glad we don't go to McDonald's. Sometimes I feel bad for the poor cows that get made in burgers. I should become a vegetation. I think that's the right word for people who don't eat animals. But it's difficult because dragons don't eat broccoli and peas.

We're sitting next to a window and I pull on mum's sleeve to show her that it has started raining. Her eyebrows shoot up into her hair. 'Wow look at it coming down. It's lucky we got inside before the heavens opened, else we would have looked like two drowned rats.'

I stroke my beautiful dress, glad that it didn't get wet in the shower. Raindrops run down the glass and I trace their path with one finger. Just when I'm thinking I might take a bite out of the table I'm so hungry, my food arrives.

Mum and Carly both steal a chip and I wave my fork at them fiercely. 'No chip thieves. These chips belong to me. Go away, you hungry seagulls.'

We went to Brighton once and a seagull knocked a packet of chips right out of another little girl's hand. They were gone in seconds. That girl screamed so loudly I thought the police would come to see what was happening.

Once I've eaten as much as I can, I let them finish the rest of the chips. I ask, 'Carly, can I have an ice-cream with chocolate sauce?'

'Please,' mum reminds me.

'Please and pretty please with a cherry on top.'

Carly opens her mouth in an O shape. 'But Maya, you didn't finish your food. You can't possibly have space for ice-cream.'

Carly thinks she's tricking me, but I have the perfect answer. 'I have two stomachs. One for food and one for pudding. Cows have four stomachs; did you know that?'

She nods solemnly. 'I did know that. But I never before heard of a girl with two stomachs. You are a medical miracle, Maya.'

'Miraculous Maya,' smiles mum, 'my wonder child.'

Carly goes to the bar to fetch more wine and to order my pudding. A man dressed as a Power Ranger comes over to our table. He's holding onto the back of a chair and swaying slightly from side to side. It is very strange to see a grown up wearing a costume when it's not Halloween. I wonder why he came to the pub dressed that way. Maybe it was a dare? When I played truth or dare with Eva, she told me to eat pepper. I threw up and it made mum very cross.

He slurs, 'Hello pretty ladies, mind if I sit down?'

Mum puts her arm around me and pulls me tight against her. 'We're actually here with someone.'

Power Ranger man doesn't say anything more, but he doesn't move away either. His suit is red and matches his face, which is also very red. Mum's fingers are digging into my shoulder and I try to wriggle away from her. Then Carly is back. She puts the drinks down on the table, nudging the strange, red man out of the way with her shoulder. As she sits down, she says, 'Run along super boy, your mates are missing you.'

He mutters something under his breath and I'm glad we can't hear what he's saying. I'm sure it was something not nice. He walks to the far side of the pub where there is a whole group of men all wearing Power Ranger costumes. I pull at Carly's sleeve. 'Why are they all dressed like that?'

'It's a stag do, baby girl. They've had too much to drink and now they're behaving like idiots.'

Mum has a frown on her face. 'It's getting pretty late. I really should get Maya home before things start kicking off in here.'

This is too much for me and I blurt, 'But I haven't had my pudding yet.'

Tears well up in my eyes, threatening to spill over. It's not fair to be promised pudding and then not get to eat it. Mum hates it when I cry. As the tears run down my cheeks, she wipes them away with a napkin.

'Don't cry, Maya. It's okay, baby, we can get ice-cream another time.'

Carly slaps her hands onto the table. 'This is ridiculous!'

She gets up and marches back to the bar. She is talking to Sam and waving her arm at the Power Ranger men. They've all got their arms around each other now and they're singing, 'You'll Never Walk Alone' very loudly and out of tune. It's such a horrible noise that I put my hands over my ears. Next thing, the men are being thrown out of the pub. They don't seem at all happy about it, but I don't care. They must go somewhere else and hurt someone else's eardrums. So, it was Aunty Carly to the rescue. Mum is smiling. She looks relaxed and happy again which means pudding is saved! I love Carly so much right then that I could squash her into a million gazillion pieces.

Mum and Carly drink wine and giggle. I eat my ice-cream which is delicious. Then I slide quietly under the table. If mum can't see me, hopefully she'll forget about heading straight home. I like the pub and watching all the interesting people. I'm not ready to leave quite yet. A man comes in with a dog. I didn't think animals were allowed in pubs. I crawl closer to Aunty Carly and whisper, 'Why does he have his dog with him?'

She looks over her shoulder, then bends down to me, 'He's blind and that's his guide dog.'

I hear mum saying, 'We really should get going, it's getting very late.'

'Ah, let's just finish this glass Sienna. Another twenty minutes won't matter either way. It's not often we get to do this.'

Aunty Carly to the rescue for the second time tonight.

I will give her the biggest kiss ever when we leave.

The dog is lying down close to our table. I click my fingers and whistle, hoping he might come over to me. He pricks up his ears and looks at me but doesn't move, his eyes look very kind. I would love to have a dog of my own. I think pugs are the cutest. Maybe Father Christmas will bring me one if I'm extra specially good. I will call her Poppy and she will sleep in my bed every night. She will be my very best friend and she won't love anyone more than she loves me. I lie on my tummy and stare at the dog. He stares back with gentle, brown eyes. We are having a staring contest. I am extremely good at staring contests; I beat mum every time. She always starts to giggle because she says I look like a serious, little owl. I'm not sure what's so funny about owls, but I like to win. So that's fine.

Lying here, I'm starting to feel sleepy. I wonder whether I should tell mum that I'm ready to go home. But the carpet is soft and the noise in the pub is suddenly like a wave. It roars but is somehow soothing at the same time. I'm just drifting off to sleep when there is a sudden shift in the air. It's not a noise or a sound. It's just a strange, hard sort of feeling. A dangerous feeling. Like impala in those nature programmes as they catch the first scent of trouble. My eyes pop open and I raise my head, scanning the room.

My eyes meet the dog's. To my surprise, he crouches and shuffles towards me. I like this game, so I do the same, getting as close to the floor as I can. His warm body is pressed against me, a comforting barrier against the bustle of the room. Then...

I hope I am an octopus.

The Lady and the Kebab

I t was no good, she thought, taxi drivers were just not as polite as they used to be. Back in the day, back in the day when she was still courting her ex, the bastard, you could do anything in the back of a cab. And once, they actually had and no harm done. But now, this bastard cab driver, bastard, swivel eyed git, wouldn't let her get in his cab just because she had a kebab in her hand. A *kebab*! I ask you! A bloody kebab! It wasn't as if it was poison. It wasn't as if she was going to make him eat it, having smeared it with *arsenic* or anything. But he wasn't having any. Locked his doors, he had, before she could get in. And driven off, nearly killed her, he could easily have killed her, driving like that. If she'd had her contacts in, she'd have taken his number, had his licence, oh yes.

She blinked. Where *were* her contacts? She could have sworn she had them in when she had left home, whenever that had been. Daylight, she knew it had been daylight then. Not like now. It was dark now and shadows made things look a bit weird. Like her feet, for instance. She looked as if she had bare feet, but one of them had this stick, this stick thing stuck to the heel. Made walking a bit difficult, except round in circles.

A kebab. She could murder a kebab. She could smell a kebab shop. Perhaps she would get one. Her friends were with her somewhere. Where were they? Was that them? No, it was some blokes, dressed in funny clothes. Wellies and pyjamas, what was that about? Oh, hang on. Her friends were there as well. Perhaps they were their boyfriends, were they? She squinted. She didn't think she knew them, but what the hell. She'd get a kebab later and a taxi, when she found her contact lenses.

Where were her contacts, anyway? Couldn't get a taxi without contacts. It was so sad, that you couldn't get a taxi without contacts. Just as well she didn't have them in because they always came out when she cried. It was all so sad.

She had a sudden idea. She'd get herself a kebab and then go home in a taxi …

A Snap of Life

Ashley Laino

Do you think it's easy keeping over a million eyes on you every day? Do you think it's easy making yourself be the object of everyone's envy and desire? Please, there is no one who works as hard as Gigi Kimberly aka Giheekygirl16 on Clickstagram. As one of the top influencers on Clickstagram, it is my job to help people know what to eat (and by eat, I mean you don't), where to vacation (as long as the location has been approved by one of my sponsors), and what waist trainers best break your ribs so you can get that natural, emancipated, tapeworm victim look.

But most of all, I am an inspiration to girls on how, if you work hard enough, maybe one day, you will be hot enough to wear a thong bikini next to your infinity pool. You too could be the jerk off material to thousands of confused, horny boys everywhere. You can make girls so jealous of your looks and your life that they develop their very own eating disorders. But it's not all fun and anal bleach treatments, if you want to be perfect online, you're going to have to put in some effort in the disgusting, real world.

For instance, I tell my followers that I start my day by waking up at 6am to make my bed. It may sound extreme, but let me tell you, once you see how nicely your house maid makes your bed after you come home at 6am after bingeing Adderall and pixie sticks all night, you really feel like you're ready to take on the day.

Once I wake up (from my two hour drug nap), it's time for breakfast. Your body is a temple and it's important to treat it as such. For example, I like my organ palace to be as empty as possible, which is why I only drink TummyShrinko tea in the morning. It has no real nutritional value, and since it has not been approved by the FDA, I'm not sure if it is entirely legal, but I do know that after five sips and one selfie holding my mug (#ad), I am in the bathroom for twenty minutes like clock work, and let me tell you, I've never felt lighter.

After my breakfast, it's time for my morning workout. I am an idol to young girls everywhere. So obviously, everyone knows that the most important thing a person could do for themselves is to beat their body into submission to obtain a physical form that is impossible for a normal working human to maintain.

I achieve this through a series of high intensity workouts, Pilates, and yoga in a room so hot no one can tell if you've achieved nirvana during savasana, or if you simply passed out from dehydration. Don't worry, I give myself a day off from working out to let my muscles heal, so I just punch myself repeatedly in the stomach throughout the day to work on those abs everyone loves so much. Of course, I always make sure to take a selfie before I begin my workout, because what is the point of exercise if no one knows you're doing it.

Today, I was in the mood for some Pilates led by Fiona Dartsmouth, a former burlesque dancer and current drinksmith (waitress) at the Penny Grabber Casino. I love Fiona's teaching style. She's enthusiastic, tough, and if you back-talk her enough she'll whip quarters at you from her apron, which she keeps on during the class so she's not late for her afternoon shift.

She's also the instructor to all the big stars in London. I mean, just this morning I was doing my crotch thrusts next to Mimi MacGee, the current head dance captain for the London Angels Prep School (Go Spams! Like the meat, not the email chains). Some people think thirty two is too old to be on a prep school dance team, but their just #ageist.

After my workout, I make my way back home using the Zoom Zoom app. I always make sure to leave a note for my drivers not to make direct eye contact with me, or I'll rate them negative stars and verbally harass them for the entire trip. Don't worry, they can't rate me poorly because obviously I'm a perfect customer, and also, I inform them that if they give me anything less than five stars, I'll call their bosses and accuse them of sexual harassment.

When I get home, it's time to start the second part of my morning routine. I hop into a shower that's bigger than your living room and made with marble more expensive than most people's mortgage payments.

My body wash is made from the clay of the Amazonian river, and it's said that at least two native tribes were eliminated to collect the clay. It makes my skin so smooth and it smells ammmmmaaaaaaazzzzziiing. Also, I like to multi-task, so I make sure to primal scream as I wash my hair, so that my hair is soft and my emotions are raw and unaddressed. It may seem like a lot just to clean yourself, but in my line of work, one clogged pore could be the end of everything.

Once my shower is over, I towel off and start my skin care routine. This process takes about two hours and thirty seven steps using the Korean skin care products I've shipped over from a K-Pop tycoon. The package said that if you follow the steps exactly for three months, your skin will look as fresh as a foetus, and you won't be able to feel human touch anymore.

I didn't have the time today, but on days, when I really want to treat myself, I go to Doctor Gilbert who provides me with Botox treatments, liposuctions for those naughty areas that exercise just can't get to (stupid toe fat) and skin transplants from face slaves who are raised below ground so their skin never experiences sun damage, or the sun period. It may cost a lot but stealing the face of an unnamed youth helps me walk away looking five years younger, and since I'm turning twenty two this year, it's really time to start prepping my skin.

After my skin care is done, then it's time to do my face and make up. I don't actually buy make up anymore because brands are constantly sending me items to try and review. Altogether, my makeup collection costs more than an American college tuition, and I slab so much of that money goo onto my face that even my own mother wouldn't be able to recognize me in a line up, and I take my first selfie of the day (with a full face of makeup).

Once my features are unrecognizable, I spend some more time doing my hair with a process that involves at least fourteen products, a straightening iron, a curling iron, and a curling straightening brush. I make sure to keep my colour looking like caramel with hair appointments every two weeks down at the salon 'G' (it's pronounced J) which was my next stop of the day. They say you should visit your salon every two weeks, but I prefer every other day, so I can eliminate any split ends before they even become split ends.

For the reasonable cost of a teacher's salary, my hair artist Bebe (it's pronounced Fefe) colours, glazes, and elongates my hair using extensions from the mane of an Arabian horse. While he works, I'm served drinks with different fruits and vegetables in. I make sure to take at least forty seven pictures and I tag Bebe in all of them, as a way of a tip. What is money compared to internet fame? Honestly, with all the clout I have been giving him, he has enough customers begging for his weirdly soft touch, and I shouldn't have to pay, but I do, *because I'm a good person.*

I was so moved by my own generosity, that I got thinking in my Zoom Zoom ride home about the effect that my online presence has on my life. Listen, I know that some people think social media is for vain narcissists, who need constant attention for minor accomplishments like eating a healthy breakfast or having perfect bone structure, but those people are just unlikable, uninteresting walruses who don't understand the platform.

The internet is where life really matters now. It's how I get my money, how I get the news, how I communicate with others, hell, it's even how I met my current boyfriend Marco.

Two months ago, Marco slid into my messages on Clickstagram with a 'sup? You hot.' After investigating his network, I discovered that Marco was a rapper/ entrepreneurial/hot guy with a trust fund which caught my curiosity. Once I learned about his incredible penthouse in London and the fact that he was hung like the horses he betted on, I was smitten.

After weeks of talking and dozens of thirst trap pictures later, we were dating and I had moved my designer luggage and Chiorgi (my Chihuahua Corgi mix. Don't forget to follow her Clickstagram page!) named Baby into his home.

Our audiences seemed to love the fact that we were dating. I mean three million people liked our first couple picture. That's more than the entire population of Albania, which I have been told by my PR team is a real country, and I need to stop mixing it with the country of Genovia, which news to me, is apparently a made up country from the *Princess Diaries* franchise.

Anyways, once Marco and I saw our united view count we simply just fell more and more in love with each other and the amount of free vodka brands were sending us. We are the perfect power couple. I mean, yes Marco does travel six and a half days out of the week and all the people he hangs out with are female underwear models, but I trust him with my life!

Of course, we always try to make time for each other in our busy schedules. So whenever Marco is home, we make sure to RSVP to the greatest parties and events, so that we can be photographed as much as possible when we are together, so that we can prove to the world that we are still the epitome of true love.

My thoughts are interrupted by the Zoom Zoom driver having the audacity to tell me that we were at my home and that I needed to leave the ride. Rude. But I'm the better person, so I leave the car, without tipping obviously, and start thinking about what I want to have for lunch.

I decided to have a beautiful salad made for me by my chef Pauline. I'm on this new diet you see, where I only have the most fresh and organic foods brought to me, I photograph these foods so much that I actually start to memorize their leaf patterns, and then I throw it all away. This way I stay chemical free and more importantly, I'm able to fit into my toddler's medium jeans. My goal is to eventually be able to fit into a baby's small.

After my delicious lunch and a line of cocaine to help with that afternoon drowsiness, it's time for me to get to work. I make my way to my office and that is when I spend the next part of my day creating the image of perfection you have today. People think my job is easy, but it's real work! First, I sit down at my laptop and page through my photos and select the most sublime images and then I filter them within an inch of their lives. It's one thing to post pictures or your face, it's another thing to have people actually know what you look like. Gross!

Next, I try and think of a catchy caption to make me seem relatable to the peasant folk and add just enough hashtags. Too many hashtags just seems desperate. Then I scroll. I scroll through the comments giving gifts of likes to my faithful followers and blocking the ogres who dare to try and bring me down. For example, gigglesnort47 had the audacity to call me 'a vain, greedy, shallow attention whore.'

Please, I don't have a greedy bone in my body. In fact, I have donated to various charities this year including: Llamas That Lay (a foundation that helps lazy llamas get back on their feet when they fall over after being tipped. Who tips llamas you ask? Well, if you have to ask, then it's probably you.) \

I also threw an amazing benefit just last month for a cause that is near and dear to my heart; Plastic for Puberty (an amazing organization that offers plastic surgery to preteens who can't afford it.) I remember being twelve and asking my parents for breast implants, and my mother telling me terrible things like 'You're still growing,' or 'You're beautiful just the way you are'. Of course, once I was old enough to sign up for my own credit card, the issue of my chest, lips, nose, brows, and shin bones were all taken care of, but I will never forget my mother's verbal abuse for as long as I shall live.

As for greedy and vain, well that's big talk from someone who, based off of their profile picture, has the skin texture of a burnt waffle. I don't get angry though. I understand that these comments come from a place of pain. Not everyone is as lucky as me to have achieved physical perfection. So instead of commenting back, I just say a little prayer for them for my current deity, the Amex Black Card, and block them.

Then I have to answer emails. Emails of all things! Like I physically have to type with my fingers. Honestly, sometimes I don't even know how I deal with the pain, but somehow I always make it through, because I am that *brave*.

I respond to new brand deals, who want me to advertise their newest mascaras and horse tranquilizers disguised as diet pills. I also get emails from my **PR** agent about what parties I should plan to attend in the next month, who I'm friends with, and a few commercial deals I have been offered.

On top of everything, as I'm working I am constantly being distracted by the needs of others, like my maid having the nerve to actually want me to lift my feet while she vacuums around me. Excuse me, I do not pay you less than minimum wage, so that I can do physical labour.

After three whole hours of work, I am absolutely exhausted, and it's time for a well deserved break. I text Marco to tell him I miss him. He doesn't respond. He rarely does, usually this doesn't bother me, but today, I found myself craving human interaction. When I get in these moods sometimes, I like to call my bank and have them read my account balance, in order to relax, but today, I wanted to go out on the town.

I own three top of the line sports cars and one red Jeep bedazzled with actual diamonds just for funsie, but I simply don't have the energy to push my foot onto the gas, so I call my third Zoom Zoom of the day. It's time to shop! I mean come on, we all need a break sometimes and after all that hard posting I did today, I needed one.

My driver drops me off at the high end London shops. I don't actually need anything, but I like to do my part in helping the economy by buying shoes worth more than what most people get paid in a week. Why? Because they're preeeeeettttttttyyyy, and trust me, shopping with me is an experience of a lifetime, and my followers want to hear (aka see) everything about it, so I make sure to photograph every second of my time. I may only wear the shoes once (an outfit repeater? What am I a monster?) But the pictures last a lifetime.

All of the sales people know me by name which I love. I assume this is because I am such a valuable customer, and not because I threw my phone at various assistants because they didn't have an item in my size.

Usually, they then offer me a beverage. I like champagne from any region other than Champagne. If they don't have what I want, that's okay! I just send someone out to immediately fetch it for me.

Then they present me items that have been specifically selected for me and display them for me like poodles in a dog show. Once I have selected the best in show, one swipe of the card later and I'm off skipping to the next store. I make sure I leave my bags with my Zoom Zoom driver.

I pay my drivers to wait for me through the whole trip and if they try to leave, I call the police and accuse them of theft and attempted harassment as is my right. Yes, sometimes they have to wait for hours, but trust me, my tips make it well worth it. Where else is someone going to tell you how to fix your hair for free!

My spree turns out to be very successful. I not only walked away with a great new pair of Louise Voltien heels, but I had also managed to score three great new dresses, a new bottle of perfume, and a Rolex watch that wasn't on sale, but was actually on the wrist of the sales manager who was helping me.

I had complimented his piece and told him that it would make an amazing gift for Marco. Then, out of the kindness of this man's heart, and not because I threw a screaming tantrum on the carpeted ground, this kind, strange man offered me his watch. What a sweetheart!

I was so excited, I immediately took a picture to send to Marco, so that he could see what an excellent girlfriend I am. As the cashier was ringing me up, I flicked through Marco's Clickstagram feeling quite smug with myself. That's when I noticed it.

Girl, after girl, after girl. Not just normal girls either, all of them I had to admit were at least somewhat acceptable looking. Arms around waists, heads nuzzled into crooks of necks, cheeks kisses. For the first time, I actually started to doubt myself. Could it be? Was there a chance that Marco could be cheating on me? I had never really been the jealous type, because I've always assumed that no man could find someone hotter than me to be with, but as I continued to swipe, I felt a clench in my stomach that I did not appreciate one bit.

I checked to see if Marco had responded to my picture, but there was nothing. I sent another text just for good measure. Time passed and there was nothing, in fact, I had not heard from Marco all day. What could he possibly be doing that was more important than me? Or who for that matter.

I clenched my phone in my hand and sighed. If Marco really was cheating on me, it's not like it would break my heart or anything. Even I knew we weren't, like, in love or anything, but this could damage my reputation.

Laugh all you want, but my entire livelihood hangs by a thread. If people stop thinking I'm desirable, happy, fun, spontaneous, and perfect then they will have no reason to follow me. I won't be a role model, I won't be a goal to aspire to, I won't be an object of desire. I would simply become a nobody. With one wrong post, I could lose my money, my home, my boyfriend, and my fame.

I sat there lost in the spiral of my thoughts, until the sales-clerk awkwardly handed me my shopping bags and heartlessly motioned for me to leave the store before security was called.

Obviously, I ignored her. I had not felt like this in ages. In fact, I had not really had to feel in a long time, and let me tell you, feelings are just plain gross. So like the absolute Amazon that I am, I swallowed those emotions down with some tasty mind pills that my therapist/psychic prescribed me and decided that instead of panicking, it was time to make a plan.

So, I snatched my bags out of that heartless clerk's hand and made my way back to my Zoom Zoom.

It was 7:15pm by the time I arrived back in the vehicle. My shopping excursion had taken a bit longer than I had planned, and I was hungry for, like, actual food.

My Zoom Zoom driver had fallen asleep in the car. So I woke them up and told them to take me to a pub a bit more than an hour down the road. It wasn't my usual five star cuisine, but there should be fewer people who know me there and I found myself craving some greasy chips, and this place had the best chips period.

We arrived at the pub at about 8:25pm based on my phone, which I only checked every five minutes. Once I had settled my driver into their spot, I made my way to the entrance as quickly as I could. It looked like a short rainstorm was about to happen and the LAST thing I needed right now was for my hair to get ruined.

Decor wise, the establishment wasn't exactly fancy, or really even memorable, but months ago after a night of clubbing, I had been dying for something to eat and stumbled into this pub. A few drinks and many fish and chips later, I was smitten. With it's dusty shelves and paper napkins, there was nothing Clicksagram worthy about this place, but the food was so perfectly greasy and salty, it was worth it and based on the crowd inside, I wasn't the only one who thought so.

I asked to be seated in a corner table because I was in no mood for fan interaction. The joke was on me though, as no one even glanced at me as I made my way to my seat. Once I settled into my corner booth I immediately ordered my fish and chips and a large pint. Calories be damned. Anyway, I'll just make it up by taking an extreme HIT PowerDestroyer KneeCracking class. Those classes were all the rage right now. They were like Crossfit classes on steroids. Your body is pushed to such physical (and mental) extremes, that if you don't cry or vomit by the end of class, they'd probably give you your money back.

With a deep breath, I glanced at my phone. It was 8:35pm and there was still no text from Marco, not even an emoji. He was definitely cheating on me. That had to be it. There was no other excuse for him not texting me back at this hour.

I could feel my face heat up, as I picked at my designer phone case, which I had bejewelled with individual crystals and gems. That asshole. He really thought he could blow me off like this and that there would be no repercussions. I was going to show him. I was going to take him down and teach everyone not to mess with GiGi Kimberly. The only question was how?

I placed my phone face down on the table and rested my hand in my cheek. Should I cheat on him? Fight fire with fire? Humiliate him first. I mean it wouldn't exactly be hard finding someone to agree to do the deed with. I could probably snap my fingers and have at least three options in this pub alone.

The restaurant servant, person, thingy placed the beer glass in front of me. I gripped the cool glass and peered over the rim around the room.

Ugh. There was no one but fuglies and trolls. In one section there was a pack of obnoxious nerds dressed as Power Rangers for some sort of stag do. At the bar, was a woman getting absolutely tanked, which I respected, but I didn't exactly swing that way, and the bartender looked absolutely miserable. Yeah, there was no way I was going to sully my lady palace with one of these rejects. There had to be another way to get my revenge.

When my food arrived, I was lost in thought still trying to think of what to do. The delicious waft of fat and grease floated towards my nostrils. Maybe I needed some calories to get my mind working more sharply.

Just as my knife was sliding into the buttery fish, I was approached by a strange man who reached out his hand. I couldn't tell at first if he was homeless, or a trendy hipster, but after he introduced himself, I learned that he was actually a member of some charity whatsit trying to get money from me supposedly for the 'Royal Society for Blind Children.'

Please, I know a scam when I see one, and based off of some of the looks from the other customers, I wasn't the only one who was annoyed at having their meal interrupted.

He was going off on some speech about 'kindness' and 'those less fortunate,' when I waved him away. Who on Earth would spend their hard earned cash on some busted kids without so much as a photo opportunity If I'm going to give my dough away, I sure as hell am going to make sure that the person in the most need is getting attention, and that person is me.

With the beggar properly shooed away, I took my first bite of my fish and chips. I hadn't had food like this in at least a year and it was pure fattening heaven. I know that this was totally going to destroy my diet, but it was worth it, and besides, I could always just throw it up later. Ditch the bloat, and that way it's almost like I get to taste it again!

I savoured my first few bites with an almost prayerlike reverence. I could actually feel my mind firing up the circuits. I checked my phone again. Still nothing. That son of a bitch. I hope Marco gets Chlamydia, and if he thinks he's going to kick me out of that sweet ass apartment, he has got one hell of a lawsuit coming. Oooooooooooh, maybe that was it. Take the bitch to court and hurt him where it really hurts, his wallet. The only thing I needed to think about was what to sue him for. Slander? Emotional abuse? Bad facial hair?

The Power Ranger boys had started to get more rowdy and drunk. The pub's stern faced bouncers are circled around them like a vulture. I took another swig of alcohol and checked my phone once again.

My heart started to pound when I saw that I had a text message, but that excitement disappeared as quickly as it came when I realized that the message is just from my old school friend Tamara checking in to see how I am. Gross.

The antics of the ranger nerd boys had reached a peak and they were soon quickly escorted out of the pub by security. Dorks. I check my phone once again, still nothing.

I returned to my meal, thinking as I enjoyed each bite. Maybe I was overthinking this, maybe he was just really busy working or buying me something expensive. What an idea! What would I look like if I was sitting here wondering on how to sneak laxatives into Marco's protein shake, and here he was buying me the extremely endangered, rare, mink, fur coat with elephant tusk, ivory buttons I had been drooling over for the past month?

I took a huge swig of beer in excitement. That had to be it! I was just being a stupid girl. My heart pounded with excitement and I waved at my bar servant to fetch me another drink.

My daddy was right. Girls are better at looking pretty then thinking pretty. Marco is such a sweetheart. I mean for our anniversary last month he bought me a custom bikini with his face on the ass. What could possibly be more romantic than that? Then here I was getting fat and plotting against him.

I didn't know if it was the beer mixing with my anxiety medication, or if I had just reached a new revelation in my life, but I was suddenly inspired to be a bit kinder to other people, maybe even consider that they may have feelings and aren't just vessels to be used at my disposal. I mean, it's a crazy idea, I know. But I was so deep in my junk food coma, anything seemed possible. I knew that the first person I had to help was Marco.

I was going to make myself the best girlfriend the world and the internet has ever known. I grabbed my phone and angled it above my head. I knew my angles. Cheekbones sharp enough to cut diamonds, high enough to hide any evidence of a double chin, lips parted just enough to draw attention to the glory of them. I mean, I didn't spend all that money on lip injections not to show them off.

While my sweetie was out most likely buying me a gift, what better present could I give him in return, then the gift of my beauty.

I sent the photo, waited a minute, and then checked my phone. Nothing. I pouted and lifted my second beer to my lips. Thankfully, some commotion from outside was able to distract me from Marco.

Apparently, the fabulous drunk woman from the bar had gotten a touch too fabulous and was now screaming something outside the pub to a taxi driver. In what seemed like slow motion, I watched her toss a kebab that she snagged from the pub at the window of the taxi driver's car. I leaned forward with excitement to see if this was going to turn into an all out brawl. I mean, recording a bar fight isn't my usual style, but it could make for some great material for my Clickstagram.

Sadly, though she was quickly surrounded by a group of people and must have been hurried away at some point because I didn't get to see her again.

Ugh, going to this seedy place seemed like a good idea when I was hangry (angry and hungry) but all these low lifes were reminding me why I haven't been to this dive in a while.

I snapped for my pub monkey to fetch me a final drink and my check. I was getting tired, frustrated, and a bit bloated. It was almost ten o'clock at night. Normally, this was the time when I started to get ready for my night, but apparently the fish and chips were not agreeing with me, so it was time to go home.

I handed the drink lackey my debit card for the meal, when the power cut out suddenly. The waitress reassured me that it was probably just a power surge. True, it was only down for a few seconds, but I took it as a sign that it was definitely time to get out of this dump.

Unfortunately, two minutes later the waitress returned to inform me that the power outage had interfered with their machines and that they would need a couple extra minutes to reboot the system.

I rolled my eyes, grateful that I had ordered another drink to keep me company while I waited on other people's incompetence. I checked my phone. There was still no Marco, but my fellow influencer Jubilee (who had significantly fewer followers than me I'd like to point out) had invited me out to the club Kings. It was the hottest night spot right now, filled with the best drinks, richest people, and most talented interpretive dancers.

Normally, I would be all over this invitation like a fly to garbage, but the bloating had turned into full on churning in my gut. I had to get home immediately.

I scanned the room for my pub maid. My check should be ready by now, but she was nowhere in sight. Instead, some weirdo had brought his dog into the pub and it was just laying on the floor like a mongrel with its tacky little vest.

Ugh, this guy. Sitting there like he needs that dog or something to guide him or something, so lame. It was probably all for attention.

Finally, after what felt like an eternity, I got my check and my card back. If this wench thinks that she's getting a tip from me after the mental torture she put me through of having to wait for my check, she is out of her mind.

I sign the receipt and slip my card back into my purse. As I got up to leave, I felt my stomach roll. Clutching my bag to my chest I hurried my way to the loo, rushing past another intoxicated woman who seems to have drunk an entire tray of beers all by herself.

There was a line for the ladies' room, of course, but everyone knows that lines don't apply to Gigi. So I busted my way to the front, ignoring the protests of the commoners behind me, and slipped into the restroom.

I will not go into detail about what bodily functions were expelled from my in that restroom, what I did know is that those girls in line could complain and knock on the door all they wanted, they were still in for a rude surprise once they made their way in here. Also, since I was in no rush, I had time to scroll through my various timelines, and was able to reconnect with the real world inside my phone.

Once I was feeling thoroughly relieved, I made my way out of the loo and passed by my haters. As I was making my way to the exit, Tipsy McGillicutty knocked over all her glasses and they crashed spectacularly onto the floor.

This brought on hoots and hollers from the other

patrons of the bar, including some obnoxious yapping from that weird old man's dog. This was it. I don't care how good the food tastes, there was no way I was ever going to degrade myself by coming to this dump again. I was Gigi Kimberly and I deserved better.

I crossed my arms with a huff, waiting once again for the wait staff to do their jobs. There was glass all over the floor and I was not going to risk my getting hurt, or worse, my designer shoes ruined.

While they cleaned up the broken glass, I checked my phone once more. But this time, there was a message on there that made my eyes widen. It was a text message from Marco. No picture, no video, just a single text message with the words "we need 2 talk" spelled out.

My heart started to pound and my hands would have started to sweat if I had not had my sweat glands removed from my hands surgically a few years back. Talk? About what? Was there something wrong? Was Marco going to break up with me?

Shoes or no shoes, I had to get out of this bar and call Marco. I had to find out what was going on. I had to make sure that this asshole was not going to ruin everything I had worked so hard to build. My online persona was spotless, and there was nothing in reality that was going to ruin my world for me.

I checked my phone one last time, 22:22, swiped it shut, and took a single step forward…

The Charity Collector

Being a charity collector had seemed a good idea at the time. Sign up for a box and shake it under people's noses and you're good to go. Meet new people, talk about the good cause – any good cause, it was easy to mug up – and then you didn't have to spend the day and night alone in a flat, looking at four walls. Slowly, the charity collecting had kind of taken over. It was almost like having a nine to five, which of course hadn't been the case for a while now. Last in, first out. It was an easy thing to say, not so easy when someone does it to you, though.

You couldn't just wear what you wanted as a charity collector – it took some thought. If you were too scruffy, people didn't believe that you were genuine, thought you were just another beggar but with a fake collecting tin. If you were too well dressed, then you had people say stupid things like

'You can afford to fill that tin yourself. Bugger off.' Yes, dressing the part was quite an art, that was for sure.

And you had to pick your venue, as well. Obviously, restaurants as such were not really allowed – no one wants to have a collecting tin stuck under their noses while they're eating a meal, especially one which had probably cost the same as a week's shopping. And pubs that just sold drink, no food, they were no good either. The people in there were either diehard drunks who just stared into their glasses and couldn't see beyond them or people who had dropped in for a quick one on the way home. No, what you needed for a good haul for the charity was a pub that served bar snacks, but upmarket ones, the kind of pub that attracted people who had a bit of spare dosh, notes for preference but change would do. Some collectors nowadays carried direct debit forms with them, but that was too much like a business deal. Appeal to their better natures, make them look good in front of their workmates or other half – that was the skill.

And keep moving – don't wear out your welcome with either regulars or the staff; you got nowhere that way. That was why, this evening, the drinkers and diners at The Whistler would be making someone's life better by putting a few coins in the tin.

Pencil Lives

Lucrezia Brambillaschi

The alarm went off in a most jarring manner that morning, although frankly all its power was rather wasted: Matthew was already awake, in fact he had been for a couple of hours at least.

Big day ahead: the nervous knot in his stomach wouldn't let him sleep properly, as usual. Instead, he'd been tossing and turning and making up all kinds of terrible scenarios in his head. Everything that could possibly go wrong he had already imagined down to the finest details in his sleepless frenzy. In a way it could even be considered comforting, because hardly anything could catch him by surprise at this point; but the anxiety it all came with was a pretty steep price to pay.

With a sigh, he turned off the alarm and rolled out of bed.

As he made himself some coffee, he tried calming

himself down, but it all had little effect. Resigned to feeling miserable for a few more hours at least, he mindlessly sat scrolling through his Instagram feed, as he did pretty much every morning while having breakfast, until all the pictures blurred together into one colourfully flat haze.

And as every other morning, at a certain point his thumb hovered dangerously over yet another shirtless picture of his ex-boyfriend. Matthew sighed, allowed himself half a second to mourn the loss of that perfectly toned body, and forced himself to put down the phone: he wouldn't give him the satisfaction of relapsing, not now and not in a million years. Thankfully, he still had a few shreds of dignity and self-respect left, in spite of everything.

By the time he was getting out of the door of his apartment, all thoughts of muscly torsos and gleaming green eyes were long gone from his mind, and he was once more completely focused on the pivotal day ahead of him.

On his way to the tube station, he passed the local bakery only just opening, and a few sleepy-eyed people going in and out of the corner shops that carelessly lined the street.

Where he lived, the town always seemed slow to wake up to a new day, almost reluctant sometimes. Away from the hectic city centre, this neighbourhood felt more like a small country town where everybody knew everybody else's business. He had chosen to live there for that reason, as well as for the obvious economic ones: as much as he enjoyed all the endless possibilities that London had to offer, it was often quite overwhelming for him, and at the end of the day he found himself craving a quiet corner to go back to. After all, he was still a simple-life country boy at heart; some things are hard to change, some habits stick all through a lifetime.

But that morning, not even the quiet of such familiar streets could slow down his racing heartbeat. It was maddening, but in a way, it made him feel more alive, more vivid, acutely aware of each drop of blood circling through his body.

Completely absorbed in his thoughts, he climbed the stairs down to the platform and boarded the usual train into town.

When he emerged from the underground station in Piccadilly Circus, the sun had broken through the clouds and illuminated the perennially crowded fountain.

Matthew breathed in hard through his nose and halted in his tracks for the beat of a moment. A performer dressed and chalked up as a Hellenic statue was staring right at him, and it actually felt like they could see right through him.

Matthew looked back into the statue's vacant eyes and he felt like he was about to spiral down into endless nothingness.

Slightly shaken up, he averted his eyes and resumed walking his own way, nervously scolding himself for getting so worked up and anxious over a simple work meeting.

A bit of nerves was forgivable and understandable, but this level of acute distress was, he thought, rather on the ridiculous side.

He was completely absorbed in his own mind and barely registered his surroundings. Well, after all, what was there to say about them? Piccadilly was much as it always was; a mess. A mess of tourists trying to find their way around to the next sight to see, crowding the walkways, jamming up at the Hard Rock Café, taking pictures even in front of Boots, because it was too British to be missed, of course. Even rather early in the morning, when the biggest rush of people had not arrived yet and most shops were only just starting to open, it was one of the busiest places in London. Rather busy for Matthew's taste, anyway.

On the other hand, in every five blissfully happy and unaware tourists, there was at least one disgruntled Londoner trying to make their way through the crowd and get a quick coffee before hurrying off to work.

He managed to get to the Bookshop after having to elbow only a couple of people and speed past three groups of tourists taking pictures, which could be considered as a very positive and promising start to the day ahead.

A quick glance at the screen of his phone told him that he had a few minutes to spare and could allow himself a cigarette – a simple pleasure, with just enough of a tint of the ill-advised and frowned upon. Never mind that it was bad for his health and quite probably would be fatal to him one day: he had always had the personality of the addict, in a way, and he didn't necessarily care about consequences, especially ones that he could not immediately see or experience. In a way, a rather silly and short-sighted way, they were not real to him. He took the last drag from his cigarette and fished the keys out of his backpack. They wouldn't be open for another hour, but for today setting the shop nice and right to welcome customers was not his responsibility for a change.

He passed through the ground floor and nodded to Cindy and Peter, drinking coffee by the counter from take-away cups, and sorting through the opening paperwork. Normally he would stop for a chat and a laugh, but that morning he was too caught up in his own head, and everyone knew why.

He climbed the stairs to the top floor, where the offices sat, neat and predictable; all the nervous energy he had accumulated, building up to that moment, was now making him feel giddy and impatient. Maybe to someone else's eyes it would not appear to be such a big deal, but he cared enough that for him that meeting was pivotal, monumental.

It was, even more so than anything else, a symbol: of his worth, of having chosen the right path in life so far, of being in the right place at the right time with the right assets, for once. His mother had always wanted him to study, become a lawyer or a doctor or something equally self-important; his family had never been rich or eminent in any way, so he understood where she was coming from. However, he had always known he could never give her exactly what she wanted for him; he hoped he could still make her proud in his own way, nonetheless.

With a heart full of wings and a mind full of hope, he knocked on the door.

He felt, more than heard, a beat of silence, the ruffling of paper, the shuffle of a chair dragged lightly on the smooth tiled floor, a few light footsteps, and then the door opened.

'Ah, Matthew, good morning!' The store manager, Helen Fairbrook, greeted him warmly. 'Sharp on time as always, aren't you? Do come in, do come in, please.'

Matthew smiled and stepped into the bright office, closing the door behind himself.

Ms Fairbrook was a slight woman with an imposing personality, of an indefinite age; she was known to be very sharp and quite demanding, and when you talked, she made sure you knew she was really listening to you.

However, Matthew did not feel as intimidated as he thought he would: he admired Ms Fairbrook and trusted her judgement; as soon as he was sitting across from her and she began talking, all the negative feelings of anxiety ebbed away from him, and he felt more serene than he had in days. He hoped it to be a good sign as to what the outcome of that meeting would be.

'So, Matthew, let's cut to the chase: I've called you here today to discuss your application, of course. You have been working with us for a year, is that correct?'

Matthew nodded; he swallowed on a dry throat.

'I have reviewed the work you've done so far, and I must say, I am quite impressed. You seem to have found yourself at ease with work and in your element straight away here, haven't you?'

She smiled a rather wolfish grin, blinding but dark at the same time, and yet, somehow, she still managed to look benevolent.

Matthew nodded again, unsure for a moment if he should add something or simply wait for Ms Fairbrook to continue.

Thankfully, she didn't leave him to wonder too long, resuming the conversation straight away.

'Now, I think you know that we value commitment and dedication, and you have shown plenty of both; you also know, I believe, that usually it's the company that offers a promotion when the employee is deemed ready to advance, and that to become floor manager a certain amount of experience is required – usually, I will be frank for you, considering especially that this is our flagship store, we look for at least a couple of years of experience with the

company. Yet, you chose to submit your own application for the position anyway.' Ms Fairbrook paused, patiently waiting for him to answer her implicit question: why?

Matthew felt his stomach drop: he didn't want to come off as conceited, he just truly believed himself to be a good fit for that role.

Slowly, without lowering his gaze, he took a grounding breath and answered truthfully: he would not throw his chance away on a whim of false modesty.

'I know very well that a year of experience is usually not enough to become floor manager, and I appreciate why that is. However, I do believe that, through dedication and passion, I have actually developed a level of knowledge – of the customers, of the books and products we sell, of the company itself – that would seem to account for about double that time of experience. I do believe that I can do the job, and I can do it well, and I think I have shown, time and time again, how much I value the opportunities I have been given here and how I always strive to make the most of them.

'If you do not believe me to be ready for this, I completely understand - I will just keep working hard and learning more, getting ready for the next opportunity.

'But if you have even so much as a vague inclination to give me this position, I can promise you that I will do whatever it takes to make sure you never come to regret it.'

Matthew fell silent, suddenly feeling short of breath and emptied out. It was not necessarily a bad feeling: he felt like he had just pleaded his case to a strict and intimidating jury, and now all he could do was wait for the verdict and hope that said jury would be a just one, too.

This time, the silence stretched out for quite a bit longer; Ms Fairbrook's crisp grey eyes never once left Matthew's warm brown ones: she looked very serious and very intent, as if she could read through his appearance, even through his words, read through all of him and uncover the very essence he guarded inside himself.

Then suddenly, completely out of the blue, her stern features broke into a surprisingly warm smile. 'I could have mentioned that I had already made my decision before you even stepped through the door this morning, but I was curious to hear how you would plead your case to me, and I'm glad I did. You see, Matthew, it's not just your words, but the way you spoke them, with such passion and conviction... You are either an incredible actor, or the very opposite of it, and I am leaning heavily towards the latter. I don't think you could ever keep your true feelings away from your face and fool anyone; you are the epitome of wearing one's heart on one's sleeve - which can be a nuisance in business sometimes, so for the future I advise caution and some dissimulation.'

It was all very well, but she still had not given him a clear answer, and he would not let himself believe slight hints: he wanted to be absolutely sure before he gave free reign to his emotions, either way.

'And now I can see you are taut and anxious to hear a clear and unmistakable answer from me,' Ms Fairbrook carried on, still smiling brightly at him.

Matthew let out a brief nervous laugh.

'Can you blame me? I really care about this, so...'

'And it does you credit, I really appreciate it, believe me,,' Ms Fairbrook added. 'I won't make you suffer any longer than necessary then: the position is yours, Matthew. Congratulations. I could not be happier to entrust you to it, I know you are going to do very well and have a great career.'

Just like that, Matthew felt all the anxiety and tension leave him in one swift gust. He had made it: he had worked hard and got what he wanted. The biggest smile bloomed across his delicate features; he could not contain it, and he would have liked to have another, stronger way of expressing his joy.

But he had never been too outgoing with his emotions, and so he just sat there with a big grin on his face, too happy to feel awkward about it.

'Thank you, really, thank you for this opportunity, it means the world to me...'

Ms Faibrook smiled knowingly as she shuffled through a folder of documents on her desk.

'Now you have a lot of work ahead of you, young man, so be prepared.' She produced a sheet of paper with thick lines of print all over it and handed it to him.

'This is the upgrade to your contract; first you will have to complete the full three months of training, of course, and then you will be officially floor manager. It is a lot of responsibilities, needless to say, which makes for a lot of long shifts and weekend calls. I'm not trying to scare you off, but just be aware that it will be tough, especially at first. But I'm sure you will get the hang of it quite quickly.'

Matthew nodded enthusiastically. 'I'm ready to do all the hard work that will be necessary, it doesn't scare me.'

He started looking through the terms of the contract as Ms Fairbrook explained details and technicalities.

They spent another half hour defining the course of his training program, breaking down all the areas that needed to be covered and such. Come Monday he would officially start as manager in training. He couldn't have been happier or prouder of himself.

By the time he got out of Ms Fairbrook's office, he felt ten times lighter than when he had stepped into it an hour earlier.

The actual work day went by quite uneventfully; all the colleagues on shift congratulated him on the promotion, and although he was very pleased by it, there was only one person's smile that he longed to see.

Colin walked in around midday to start his shift, hair quite dishevelled by the wind that had picked up during the morning, rosy cheeks and full, red bitten lips.

Every time he saw him, Matthew felt his knees threaten to give out suddenly – which was such a silly schoolboy reaction, but he couldn't even bring himself to be embarrassed about it, especially not today.

Colin smiled and waved at him as he walked past the tills towards the staff room; he was always sweet and nice to everyone, and Matthew was always afraid that he imagined the increased brightness of his smile and lingering blue eyes on him when Colin saw him.

All the same, he couldn't wait to tell him the news, and maybe use it as an excuse for celebration, for going somewhere together; he felt more daring than he ever had before, still on a kick from the good news of the day.

He waited for Colin to join him behind the tills, quite distracted and dazed; he kept serving customers as they turned up, but he felt like he was in a dream, suspended and surreal. He should not get his hopes up: Colin was widely considered a very handsome guy, and rightfully so; on top of that, he was such a kind and considerate person that everyone had a little bit of a crush on him. He'd started working at the Bookshop two months before and he'd been stealing hearts ever since; the most endearing part was that he didn't even seem to notice it.

But Matthew also knew that Colin was said to have a fling with Susie, a young secretary that worked in the offices on the top floor, which was a clear sign of how much he should not get his hopes up.

But one never knew, in these situations: no matter how you tried to stamp it down, hope always had a way of rising back up and getting its voice heard.

So caught up was Matthew in his own thoughts that he didn't even notice that Colin was already beside him until he heard his slightly raspy voice.

'That's £15.70, please. Do you need a bag, Madam?'

With a start, Matthew realized he had been completely zoning out while shuffling over and over again a pile of the new gift cards they had just received. He shook his head, trying to wake himself up to reality. Thankfully, the shop was very quiet at the moment.

Colin waved goodbye to the customer and seamlessly turned to him with a blinding grin on his lovely, lovely face.

'So, I've heard the big news! Congratulations, dear.' He playfully winked at Matthew.

Matthew felt a blush creep up his neck; he loved when Colin called him *dear*, but he also hated it, because of how it reduced him to a blushing, bumbling mess, and it gave him hope that he felt he was not entitled to. Colin was sweet and a bit cheeky with everyone, after all.

Matthew cleared his throat, his hands still nervously playing with the gift card.

'Yes, uhm, thank you....'

He trailed off, unsure of what to say or what to do with himself; he realized just then that he had been smiling like an idiot ever since he had heard Colin's voice.

Great, way to be charming and effortless, Matthew.

Colin's smile became even wider, and Matthew didn't even know how that was possible; the hint of a dimple was showing now, only the slightest dip of skin, but all the same Matthew thought he might just faint.

'It's amazing, you deserve it big time! And I believe that calls for celebration, don't you think?'

Colin cocked one eyebrow up and leaned with an elbow on the counter.

'Oh, yeah, sure!' Matthew said breathlessly; he mentally cursed himself and tried to calm down with a deep breath.

'We could, uhm, go out for a drink, maybe? That would be nice... Maybe we can tell some of the others as well: John, Amanda, Steve... Susie, and - '

He tried to gauge Colin's reaction at the mention of Susie's name, but his face did not change at all, and he interrupted Matthew straight away.

'Sure, if that's what you want... Or we could go out alone, just the two of us.'

Colin winked at him, he legitimately *winked* at him, with a smile that could have caused all the lightbulbs in the shop to short circuit.

Matthew swallowed, his heartbeat picking up erratically.

'Oh. Well, I mean, I... I'd love that,,' he said quietly, not trusting his voice to properly speak up.

Colin's smile widened.

'Great! We can meet here after closing time, I know a good pub nearby. Can't wait, darling,,' he added with a flirty glance, before turning his attention back to the customers approaching.

The rest of Matthew's shift went by in a hazy flurry; the shop became quite busy, Matthew and Colin didn't have much of a chance to speak again. But every time Colin caught his eye, Matthew could not help but smile and blush a little, and the fact that Colin always smiled back filled him with such giddiness that he could hardly contain.

He could not believe that Colin had asked him out, the two of them: alone, like a proper date. Oh, it was hard trying not to get his hopes up *now*.

The end of his shift rolled around before he knew it; Matthew changed and picked up his backpack from the office, waved everyone goodbye and made especially sure to walk by Colin's station, close enough that he could drop him a smile intended only for him without the whole shop noticing - at least he hoped so. He didn't want gossip stirring up before anything actually happened, especially since everybody knew he had the silliest crush on Colin.

'See you later, then.'

Colin looked up from the till and threw him a smile.

'Absolutely, darling.'

Matthew only hoped that the people around him could not actually hear his heartbeat, loud as it was. He waltzed out of the Bookshop, feeling light and bright and impossibly full of life.

'Oh, there he is, bright as sunshine! I think I already know how it went today,' his sister greeted gum as soon as he stepped out onto the street. Tall and slim, she was casually leaning against the wall, wearing her usual crisp black suit and black sunglasses.

He hopped over to her and hugged her tight.

'I got it, Liz! And not just that! I'm… Actually, I'll tell you later, let's go.'

He ushered her on towards the tube station. She laughed and let him steer her on.

'What?! I wanna know everything, come on, don't make me dig for it.' She paired her statement with a pointy jab of her fingers into his side.

He jumped back with a light squeal and shook his head, casting a meaningful glance over his shoulder back towards the Bookshop.

But she wasn't having any of his secrecy.

'It's about the cute co-worker, isn't it? What's his

name…?' she said way louder than necessary.

Matthew almost slapped his hand over her mouth to shut her up. 'Liz, *please!*'

She laughed ever harder at the clear distress in his voice. 'Okay, okay, keep you secrets… for now.'

While they took the train, Matthew started telling her all about the meeting with Ms Fairbook, relating down to the finest detail and reporting every bit of the conversation, word for word.

When she wanted to, Liz could be the best audience possible to tell a story to; she would gasp and clap her hands and exclaim in all the right moments.

By the time they had changed trains and arrived at Liverpool Street station, he was little more than halfway through his story.

'And then she finally said yes!' Matthew said to wrap up the story, just as they approached the Art Gallery where Liz worked.

'Wow, she did make you sweat for it, didn't she?' Liz said with a smile. 'But of course she would give it to you, you work harder than anyone, you deserve it. So, what are you doing tonight to celebrate? You must have something planned.'

He felt himself blush and heard his voice starting to stutter, faltering a little.

'Well, in fact…'

Liz dramatically turned to him, stopping right in front of the door, hand on the knob, and suggestively raised an eyebrow at him. 'Yes?'

Matthew sighed: he knew very well he wouldn't get out of this without telling her.

'… Colin invited me out for drinks tonight.'

'Colin is the cute colleague you have been drooling over and blabbing about for a month and a half, right?'

Matthew winced but couldn't really say she was wrong: it sounded like a painfully and shamefully accurate depiction of his behaviour, actually.

'Yes.'

Liz literally screeched with glee and triumph.

'Ah-ha! I knew something more was up with you!'

She paused in her remarks just to carefully go through the messy contents of her handbag, looking for the keys to the gallery.

She sighed, unsuccessful, and fished her phone out instead.

'Give me one second... '

She absent-mindedly chewed on her lower lip as she looked through her contacts and finally put the phone to her ear.

'Kate, it's me. I think I left my keys inside, could you – ?'

Before she even finished the question, she heard the key turning in the lock; the door flung open, revealing a stern looking 40-something woman. Matthew had known Kate for a few years, yet to this day he found her almost black eyes and sturdy figure quite intimidating. But he knew that deep down she was actually a rather sweet and generous person – just not a very outgoing one.

'You couldn't ring the bell?' Kate asked in her surprisingly mellow voice. When she was younger, she had been a singer at some point, and quite a promising one too. Matthew did not know exactly what happened, but something must have put an early and quite definitive end to her career; he had never asked for the details, but he had a feeling it had been quite traumatic for Kate.

'Oh, you know I don't like ringing the bell, it makes me feel like a visitor.'

Liz hurried inside, already switching to her work mindset, eager to have everything efficiently done and perfectly organised. Matthew followed her inside, smiling at Kate and curiously throwing glances around; it had been a while since he'd last been in the Gallery, and he knew they had been changing direction with the exhibitions they had been hosting lately: they were now more focused on works by women artists, often very politically minded, which had created quite the buzz around the Gallery. Liz really liked that kind of publicity, she said it made them stand out – which, in a place like London, was the first thing any business needed to do in order to survive, let alone thrive.

That day they were seeing to the last details for a new exhibition opening the next day; Matthew was very excited to see what it would all be about, since Liz had been so excited when she'd told him about it. He walked across the entrance into the main room, where Liz was walking around checking the collocation of the artworks on the wall, and Kate was taking notes on a tablet as her eyes carefully scanned every detail.

Liz turned around to Matthew and smiled broadly. 'What do you think then?'

Matthew stepped forward and looked around at the spacious white room, completely bare except for the pictures lining the wall.

They seemed to be mostly pencil drawings; the first thing that caught his eye was how sharp they looked, both in the colours and in the lines: there was nothing uncertain or shy about them. And they all depicted naked bodies, which made this boldness even more interesting and magnetic. Matthew felt very drawn to this type of art: it made him feel powerful and courageous, vicariously so perhaps, but it was a very welcome feeling, nonetheless.

'Oh Liz, this is so great! I think it might be my favourite out of all the exhibitions you have put together so far.'

Liz looked so proud; she always valued the opinions of her baby brother. 'I knew you would like these pieces.'

'So you're opening tomorrow?'

'Yes, and we have already been contacted by some very interested buyers. I think it's going to be a success, and the press already seems very interested as well. Oh, and I'm happy you came today because the artist herself is coming round in a bit to sort out a few last minute things, and I want you to meet her. She's great, we've been working closely with her and I love what came out of the collaboration. You're gonna love her.'

Liz was talking so fast one could barely keep up with her, as she had a tendency to do whenever she was really excited.

Matthew beamed at her, so happy for her success: he knew how important this job was to her, how it had always been her dream; he knew how hard she'd worked for it, and he could not think of anyone in the world who deserved more to have each of their dreams come true. She had always been his best friend and his closest confidant as well as his sister, and he was elated to see her so proud of her achievements.

She threw an arm over his shoulders and hugged him tight.

'I'm so proud of you, sis' he said hugging her back tightly.

Around half an hour later, the doorbell rang and a colourfully dressed woman strolled in; she moved fretfully, darting her eyes around without ever letting them settle on anything, like a squirrel looking for food in the slow waste of autumn leaves brushed about by the wind.

'Hello, Elizabeth, dear, so nice to see you, you look lovely. Oh, I love how you have arranged things, oh yes, absolutely lovely, just how I had imagined it, marvellous.'

She spoke just like she moved, jumping from one word to the next without ever committing to any.

It had been a very long time since Matthew had heard anyone call his sister by her full name, probably since her school days, but she didn't seem to mind at all.

She was looking at the woman with warmth, and Matthew could tell straight away that Liz really admired her. 'Welcome, Judy. I'm happy that you like what we've done with the exhibition so far; I still want to go over a couple of details with you… Oh, but first, let me introduce you to my dear brother Matthew. Matty, this is the woman behind the art, Judy Fae.'

Matthew nodded and extended his hand to her.

'Very nice to meet you, Ms Fae.'

She took his hand in both of hers, and for the first time since she entered the room she fixed her eyes on him, giving him her full, undivided attention. It was an experience in and of itself, the intensity her eyes conveyed made him feel like he was being held underwater: the rest of the world sort of dimmed away, and he felt extremely aware of his own existence in the physical world. It lasted barely a minute, but it felt like a century and it left him gasping for air.

She let go of his hand and let her eyes dart around the room again. 'I like the energy coming off you, young man, I like your energy,' she said as if she was talking to her artwork – perhaps she was.

She must have been the most intense person Matthew had ever met and he liked her instantly.

He hung around while Liz and Judy Fae discussed the last arrangements and changed a few things in the layout of the exhibition; he took his time to admire the pictures more closely, letting himself be captured by the details.

He was mesmerized, completely captivated; the power of art, of any kind, is that it creates a world of its own in which to exist, one that often makes more sense than the real one, and it whisks you away into it if you let it. It's the blessing of art, and the curse of those who live in it so intensely.

Almost an hour went by without Matthew even realizing; he found himself completely engrossed in a portrait of a man, abandoned on a chair, looking out into the unspecified distance. It felt so personal, as if he was intruding not only on the privacy of that man, but also on his soul, his most intimate thoughts and feelings, hopes and fears. He felt dirty, somehow, guilty; but he couldn't stop.

'It makes you feel exposed, doesn't it.'

Judy Fae's voice startled him; he turned around and found her standing right behind him, staring fixedly at him. He could not say how long she might have been there.

He nodded, unsure of what else he should say.

'I could tell from your posture, you look like you're trying to protect yourself – your core – from something. The question is: what?' she added after the briefest silence.

Matthew laughed nervously: he had a feeling that Judy noticed even more than she let on; he also sort of believed her to be psychic or something like that.

She kept looking at him for a few seconds more, then nodded to herself. 'Yes. I like your energy.'

She turned around and walked away towards the office, leaving him confused but intrigued.

He had already turned back to the picture when he felt, more than heard, her steps come to a halt before she reached the other room.

'What would you say to modelling for a piece?'

Matthew turned back to her, even more confused, thinking she must have been talking to someone else – but there were only the two of them in the blinding white room, and once again her piercing eyes were trained on him.

'I… uhm, me? Oh, I never thought I'd… Yeah, I guess, why not,' he agreed tentatively, with the distinct sensation that he had no real idea what he was getting himself into. Nevertheless, he was intrigued, even more so than he was confused and surprised.

Judy did not seem fazed or surprised in the least; she just nodded solemnly once more and went back to her own business.

Matthew didn't turn back to look at the picture again: he was afraid that, if he did, he would see his own likeness in the sharp pencil lines.

Judy Fae left shortly afterwards, in a sudden whirlwind exactly as she had arrived; all of a sudden, the place felt intrinsically empty and quiet.

Liz approached Matthew with a rather enigmatic smile plastered on her face. 'She left this for you.'

She handed him a torn and half-crumpled piece of paper with a number and an email address hastily scribbled on it in red pencil.

Matthew took it and turned it around in his hands, still too stunned by the encounter with Judy Fae to fully realize what had happened or feel any particular way about it – embarrassed, normally he would feel embarrassed and self-conscious about it.

'Oh yes, she asked me to pose for her and I accepted,,' he simply noted with a rather flat voice.

Liz's smile widened.

'I thought she might.'

Matthew looked up at her and shook his shoulders.

'Yesh, it was… weird. Good weird, though. Whatever. How about we go for something to eat? I'm starving. Too many strong emotions today.'

They said their goodbyes to Kate and walked to the tube station, headed for a restaurant on the South bank of the Thames, where they served one of the best and most generous afternoon teas in London.

The sunlight was blinking and shining on the water as if the surface of the river were encrusted with a hundred thousand tiny diamonds. They asked for a table on the terrace and sat down enjoying the warm afternoon light.

'So? Where is Prince Charming taking you tonight then?'

Matthew threw his sister a sideways glance.

'He's not… Ugh, I don't know, we are to meet in front of the Bookshop later – he's closing – he said he knows a place near Piccadilly to have a few drinks… But it's just a friendly celebration between colleagues, totally innocent, so don't get your hopes up,,' he hastily added.

Liz burst into laughter.

'Okay? Are you trying to convince me or yourself?'

Matthew shrugged. He was trying to keep his own excitement at bay, which was his usual approach to life when he was scared of being let down and getting hurt. 'I'm just saying - I don't know, okay? It's fine, it's just…' he trailed off rather conspicuously.

He was babbling nonsense and he was acutely aware of it.

Liza gracefully dropped the subject for the moment instead of torturing him further – as she would have done up until a handful of years ago, teasing him mercilessly for her own amusement. Thankfully, they were all grown up now.

They steered towards more pleasant and neutral topics of conversation as they ate the little assorted sandwiches and delicious buttery bites.

Inevitably, they ended up talking about the Gallery again, and of course Judy Fae.

'So, the youngest floor manager, heartbreaker, and

now even art model?' Liz said lightly. 'I am actually pretty impressed, Matty. Have you told Mum already? She will be thrilled… about the promotion. About the modelling bit, not so sure, but what can you do, she's a mum.'

Matthew shook his head and sighed.

'I'll call her tomorrow and tell her about everything, I promise.'

If he'd called her straight away, he would have ended up telling her about the whole Colin thing as well (because he was physically unable to keep anything from his mum) and she would have grilled him for ages about it until his anxiety would skyrocket. She didn't do it on purpose: like Liz said, she was a mum.

Liz nodded, understanding perfectly where he was coming from.

'Well, then,,' she said resolutely, lifting up her glass full of light bubbly Prosecco. 'To my successful, beautiful little brother – may all your dreams come true, and may this Colin guy turn out to be filthy rich so you won't have to work another day in your life.'

Matthew laughed.

'He's working part-time at the Bookshop to pay for Uni, so I have my doubts about him being rich, but I appreciate the sentiment.'

They toasted and laughed and spent some more lovely time together, without a care in the world, while the sun slowly sank lower in the sky and the buildings around them cast shadows on the water.

He got to Piccadilly Circus just a handful of minutes before Colin finished his shift.

He lit up a cigarette and leisurely walked to the Bookshop entrance, settling to wait just outside. He was feeling rather nervous, his heart beating too fast; he didn't want to go inside, hoping that the cool evening air and some nicotine would help calm him down a little.

Just a few minutes later, he heard the key turn in the door, and then Colin was standing right there, slightly dishevelled, eyes bright as they landed on Matthew; when he talked, his voice sounded excited and just raspy enough to drive Matthew a little bit crazy already.

He was gorgeous.

'Hello stranger. Hope you didn't have to wait long. Let me just lock everything up and I'll be all yours.'

He gave him one of his signature winks before turning back to the door and Matthew felt his unruly heart skip a couple of beats.

'Here we go! So, did you celebrate this afternoon?' Colin asked as they started walking towards Brewer Street and Soho.

Matthew smiled nervously; he did not want to act like an awkward teenager on his first date, because he really liked Colin and wanted a chance to get to know him better, at least. But that was precisely why he felt so nervous. He took a short breath and prayed not to make a fool of himself during the night.

But at some point, he had to let go of all these fears and insecurities, and just – be.

'Yeah, I spent some time with my sister Liz. I always love spending time with her, we're very close,,' he blurted out before the nerves could get the best of him.

'Oh, that's lovely! I wish I had any siblings, but my parents have always been of a different mind… One unruly son was enough for them, I guess.'

He seemed very thoughtful and serious as he mentioned his parents, as though a cloud was darkening his brow. But the moment passed before Matthew could really grasp it, and Colin was back to his light and bubbly self. 'Is she older or younger, your sister?'

'She's older, yeah, four years older. She's always looked out for me, in a way…'

Colin gushed. 'Aw, that's so cute, it must have been nice for you. She must be very proud of her successful young brother then!'

Matthew blushed at that, but he was pleased by Colin's remarks.

'Yeah, she's happy for me… You know, I'm very proud of her too: she manages an art gallery near Shoreditch and organizes these super cool exhibitions, mainly of women artists. You should totally come and check out the latest one, it's opening tomorrow. I have a feeling you would like it.'

For some reason, he was suddenly feeling very brave: maybe the confidence radiating from Colin was kind of rubbing off on him.

'Oh, I'd love to,,' Colin remarked with a big warm smile. 'Maybe we could go together some day.'

Matthew nodded and smiled back, feeling the proverbial butterflies go crazy in his stomach.

He followed Colin into a lively pub; he just had enough time to glance up and read the name – 'The Whistler' – before a crowd of cheery people engulfed them. He tried to stick as close to Colin as possible as they made their way inside towards the bar.

There weren't many free tables, but Colin scanned the room thoroughly until he spotted a nice small place, quite tucked away from the chaos of the main floor; he grabbed Matthew's wrist and leaned in close to his ear to make his voice heard over the noise.

'Go and sit down, I'll get the drinks and join you. What would you like?'

'A cider, apple cider.'

He felt the emptiness left on his skin when Colin's fingers slipped away, and all he could think of as he struggled to reach the table before anyone else sat at it was how much he wanted Colin's hands back on him as soon as possible.

Matthew sat down and looked around at the other people in the room while he waited. There were all sorts of different people, couples, groups, older, younger, quieter, louder. London always offered such diversity: you really felt like you could disappear into the crowd, no matter who you were or what you looked like, because you would hardly ever stand out in such a heterogeneous crowd. Matthew found it a comforting thought for the most part: he had always been quite shy, and he never really liked being at the centre of attention. This chance at anonymity and invisibility was one of the things that had drawn him to London the most.

He saw Colin reappear through the crowd, balancing

two pints and two shot glasses on a tray. He set it all down on the table and squeezed into the booth next to Matthew.

'Here you go, darling, here's your cider. But first, I thought, what kind of celebration would it be without a nice tequila shot?'

He passed the small glass to Matthew, a wedge of lime balanced on the rim. He took Matthew's hand in his and turned it around to sprinkle a pinch of salt just between the base of his thumb and index; Matthew felt delicious electricity spark where their skin touched.

Colin took some salt on his hand as well, then looked him in the eye and raised his own glass.

'To the youngest and prettiest floor manager any bookshop has ever seen.'

Matthew giggled and blushed, but he felt too happy to care.

He looked Colin lick the salt off his own hand and had to remind himself how to breathe properly. He quickly followed suit and downed his shot, flinching just a little at the burn of alcohol and the bitter taste of lime. He could feel warmth spread through his body, smooth and constant, but he wasn't sure if it was from the alcohol or rather from Colin's body almost pressed against his own in the cramped space.

They started talking a little about work, but quickly moved away from it and switched to more personal topics.

In spite of how nervous he had felt, Matthew soon discovered that talking with Colin was much easier and much more comfortable than he had anticipated: he looked at him with such deep eyes that seemed ready to drink all of his up, but at the same time he did not feel pressured to be a certain way or act a certain way. He felt seen and listened to, he felt wanted and appreciated just as he was.

Somehow the conversation veered on films, and Matthew found out that Colin was very passionate about cinema and quite impressively knowledgeable; the way he talked about it lit his eyes up, and Matthew found himself thinking that he could have looked at him forever and been perfectly happy. He hung on Colin's every word, followed his every inflection, and couldn't help admiring the elegant and slightly angular curve of his jaw, the unruly curl that kept falling on his forehead, the slight dip underneath his lower lip.

Matthew was completely enthralled, the world around him only a rather distant background; he was so focused on Colin's voice and Colin in general that he hardly noticed the noise around, or anything else going on in the pub.

He could not have said how long they spent deeply in conversation with each other, like the world began and ended in the words they exchanged.

At some point Matthew noticed that both their glasses were empty; he gestured to them as he stood up.

'My turn. The same?'

Colin nodded and flashed him a smile that engulfed his eyes with warmth. Matthew was sure he had never seen a prettier boy in his entire life.

He once again elbowed his way towards the bar and ordered their drinks.

While he was waiting, he took a moment to look around himself and observe his surroundings. The pub looked pretty much like any other London pub; on the wall in one corner he noticed a rainbow flag, a nice reminder that they were still in Soho after all.

Once the bartender handed him the drinks on a tray, Matthew gingerly stepped back towards the table, trying to balance the tray properly, hoping not to spill anything on anyone.

Somehow he managed to reach their table without messing up. Column cheered him on in a ridiculous and exaggerated manner, and they both burst into laughing for no real reason other than they were young and happy and maybe slowly falling for each other a little - or a lot.

Matthew thought that life had never been kinder to him than it was being that day.

And maybe it was all the good things that had happened during the day, or maybe it was the second shot of tequila he had just gulped down, or maybe it was the way Colin was looking at him, so bright and raw and deep and intimate - whatever the reason, Matthew was suddenly feeling audacious.

With a smile he couldn't quite hide, he slowly leaned into Colin's side; it was almost imperceptible to an untrained eye, but between them the electric currents spiked and sprinkled like crazy fireworks.

He heard Colin breath in a little too sharply, and the distance between their faces – between their lips was now slight like the fluttering of butterfly wings.

Matthew slowly let his eyelids flutter shut and anticipated the moment in which his lips would meet Colin's, only a delicate brush at first, and then a more intimate touch.

He felt Colin's breath warm up the skin of his upper lip.

Maybe heaven was a kind of slow kiss.

One Man and His Dog

People often asked him why he went out at night with his dog and his answer was always 'Why not?' He didn't ask them why they went shopping on a Saturday morning when they had the rest of the week to do it. He never asked them why they always mowed their lawns on a Sunday morning when people were trying to have a lie in, or why they had a bonfire or a greasy barbecue just as people's washing was going on the line. People always thought it was okay to speak to him as if he were a child or a little simple minded. But in fact, as he often pointed out, he couldn't see. And that was it. End of.

He had never discussed it with his dog, they weren't really on those kind of terms. When he was a child, they had never had a pet, not after the unfortunate incident with the goldfish and his grandfather's dentures, anyway – his excuse was he was very little and the goldfish looked bored. No excuse, really, but that was the end of pets. So when he lost his sight and was promised a dog, he didn't turn cartwheels. He and the dog had a working relationship, as he saw it – he fed the dog, the dog made sure he didn't go under a bus. And it worked pretty well.

This particular evening, he thought he might push the envelope a bit and go somewhere new. It wasn't any good asking the dog to choose, of course – it was good at a lot of stuff, but reading pub names wasn't in its skill mix, really. But still, if he could attract the attention of a passer-by, most of them were polite enough to answer what he asked. He had come up short with a stag do earlier in the evening. He could tell there were six or seven of them, pissed as owls apart from one, who seemed to be in charge. Designated driver, he supposed; if only they knew how much he would give to have the job again, though it had annoyed him enough, back in the day.

The dog had taken him to the threshold of several pubs as they set out from the Tube. One was louder than Hell, some band yelling inanities from a stage at the far end and he knew that would freak out the dog as well as driving him potty. Another smelled of … well, he wasn't sure, but the dog was huffing and sneezing, backing out as much as a guide dog would ever do that. So he walked on a little further.

He felt the pavement change and he knew another pub was nearby. Hearing footsteps, he took a pace forward and said, 'Excuse me, could you tell me the name of this pub?'

The man stopped on a wave of aftershave so strong it made him blink. Did women really go for that?

'The Whistler,' the man said, unexpectedly. When he had smelt the aftershave, the blind man had assumed that the other was on a promise and would have no time for him. 'Would you like me to take you in? The doorway's a bit narrow and …' Like most people, he stopped, embarrassed.

'Thank you. That's very kind.'

'Not at all,' said Aftershave Man. 'After you.'

Chance

Samantha Evergreen

Today

The vibration from Cassie Arantes' phone would have woken anyone. She groaned as she rolled over in her bed, forced her brown eyes open and looked out of her window to find the sun just starting to peek over the London skyline, the sky alight with pastels of pink and yellow just starting to deepen into the early morning. She looked over at her alarm clock and found it was only six am.

Cassie rolled her eyes hoping it wasn't work calling her in as she looked over at her bedside table with narrowed eyes to where her phone sat. The screen was lighting up with a bright blue and Cassie could see that she had received a text. Letting out a breath she reached over and picked up her phone and unlocked it to open the new message.

'Hey, you want to get some coffee with me?'

Cassie bit down on her bottom lip to keep from smiling but still she felt her mood rising as she read the name at the top of the screen. It was from Dylan. She didn't wait a moment before she quickly typed out a text and hit send.

'Race you there.'

Cassie let her phone fall into her light blue sheets then, swinging her feet out of bed. She took a quick shower before heading to her wardrobe. Opening the door, she looked at her meagre selection of clothing. It was mostly muted colours, that didn't really go with how she felt and the nice weather they had today. She needed something bright and cheerful.

It took her a few minutes of digging but, finally, she found a pink shirt and light blue jeans. She threw them on and stepped into some white flats before going to put on a little makeup. It wasn't much but it highlighted her features, with a rose-coloured lipstick and cream-coloured eyeshadow. In a way, she felt like a teenager again getting ready for her first big date and wasn't sure why. She had been seeing Dylan on and off for three months now... but today she just felt like looking a little special.

Not even fifteen minutes later Cassie felt her heart racing as she basically ran down the street and hoped she didn't look that crazy as her breath came out in heavy pants as she turned the corner, but had to stop suddenly as the traffic light in front of her turned green.

She looked up and moved a piece of her blonde hair out of her face as cars zoomed past her and as she caught her breath she looked around herself. It was a flawless summer morning, the sun shining down warming her pale skin, not a cloud in the blue morning sky, it was the storybook perfect day. People milled all around her even though it was only six-thirty in the morning. But that was life when you lived in the heart of London.

For most of her life, Cassie had lived in Forest Hill but had moved to Soho a year ago now to work at St Thomas's Hospital as a nurse. Her parents hadn't been happy with her move because Soho had had a bad reputation for years, being seen as a pretty seedy place to go in the capital to get porn and watch smutty films, along with sex workers at night, not a place many would want their daughters living in, at least in her parents' eyes. But that had been a long time ago and now it was known as one of the main entertainment districts, with shops of every kind you could think of, bookshops, clothing and shoe stores and even high-class restaurants. Not to mention Chinatown being only a walk away and of course, the Prince of Wales' Theatre was a draw for tourists.

But even with all the people buzzing around, Cassie was thankful she had picked today to have her day off, not only for the nice weather but because Dylan had also decided to take the day off too and he had probably been out for a run when he had texted her.

She spotted him across the street then at the little cafe they always met up at when they could and she couldn't help the smile that spread across her lips when she saw what he was wearing. The navy blue shorts that made her heart beat that little bit faster. His brown hair waving around his face as a breeze kicked up suddenly making him look like some kind of model, at least to her he did.

The sign that told her and the others who waited turned green then and she quickly crossed the street and hoped her face didn't show the delight she felt as she walked over to where he stood buying a cup of coffee.

She got in line just in time for him to turn away from the ordering window to face her, cup in hand. 'You cheated,' Cassie said.

'You had time, I only got here five minutes ago,' Dylan said with his classic half-smile, his lips turning up on the right side as he looked at her.

'You know I'm not a runner,' Cassie said, as she moved up in line and told the women working there her order of one black coffee before she moved to the side to wait with him, 'I get short of breath at jogging let alone running.'

He smiled as he rolled his eyes at her, 'Cassie, I've seen you run across the hospital in a minute so don't try that with me.'

'Whatever,' Cassie said but she was smiling too.

'The weather really is amazing today,' he said, taking a drink of his coffee.

'Right, a day off and a sunny day to spin out in London. It's like the stars aligned for us in some kind of way.'

'I know. I'm not sure we'll get another day like this again.'

'You mean a day off?' Cassie asked as she took her coffee from the women before they moved to one of the tables and sat down in a shady nook.

'No, a day like this. Perfect weather, a good cup of coffee, and now you; couldn't happen again, could it?'

Cassie looked down, biting her lip. 'Well, it's not like the stars have to align for you to see me,' she said, taking a long drink from her coffee.

Dylan looked down at his own coffee a moment before he spoke. 'Cassie, I enjoy these moments with you so much, you really have no idea.'

'Well, that's good to hear; I was worried there you hated our time together,' Cassie said with a sarcastic smile and she watched as his lips turned up.

'I know what you want and I...'

'And you what?' Cassie asked softly, looking him in the eye now, wanting him to see what she wanted him to say to her. They had been on and off for so long now, and she was never sure what this was to him. A hook-up? Or something more?

'You know as well as I do that we both –' His words were cut off suddenly as both their phones started ringing.

Cassie closed her eyes a moment knowing this perfect day was over. Knowing their time together was over, for now at least.

She reached into her bag and pulled out her phone at the same time he did.

'Hello?' Cassie answered, already downing her coffee as fast as she could.

'Sorry to call you in on your day off but we need all hands on deck today. There was a big pile up on the Strand and A&E is packed; would you be willing to come in?' Mary, the head of nursing, asked her.

'Shit,' Cassie breathed as she looked up and met Dylan's green eyes. They both knew their day off was over because they both loved their jobs, helping people was what they were meant to do and they knew it.

'I'll be right there,' Cassie said before she hung up. She got up and so did Dylan.

'Well, isn't that just great,' Dylan said, putting his own phone away.

'I'll get the cab,' Cassie said and went over to the sidewalk and a moment later a black car stopped in front of her.

She looked back at Dylan and without another word, they got in and headed for the hospital.

It wasn't a long drive, thank God. Cassie wasn't sure she could have taken being in the too-quiet car much longer. The things they wanted to talk about weren't something you said with a stranger listening in, so instead, they sat there in silence, their fingers lacing together.

Finally, the cab parked and they both jumped out and made their way through the staff entrance.

Cassie paused, her hand on the door to the female locker room as she looked back at Dylan, both feeling that this day still wasn't over for them.

'What happened to you?' Alice asked as she put on her scrubs.

'We met up again,' Cassie said, the disappointment clear in her voice even if she didn't mean for it to be, as she opened her locker and got out her own set of scrubs.

'Oh, Cass you really shouldn't have, you know what they say about work relationships. '

'And what's that?' Cassie asked a little bitterly, pulling up her trousers.

'They work or they don't, it ends well or with one of you quitting.'

'Thanks,' Cassie said sarcastically, rolling her eyes before she headed out into A&E.

Cassie had imagined her first year as a nurse hundreds of times over the course of the twenty-four years of her life. Growing up, she'd spent as much time in hospitals as she did out of them with her epilepsy that she thankfully had under control now. But when she had been ten, she'd started wanting to know the details about what was happening to her and why it happened.

She had pored over books and the internet, asking her parents all kinds of questions, but they didn't always have the answers so she pursued medicine because she wanted to be the person with all the answers, and after years of nursing school she'd finally been ready.

The first seven months on the wards had been going fine, that was until Dylan got there. In his thirties, he was the head radiographer on the third floor.

It had been a weird day when they first met one that shouldn't have even happened in the first place. But it had.

Three months ago.

'Damn it, Cassie, get up,' Mary had barked at her then.

Cassie barely had got to sleep when she opened her eyes and robotically swung her legs off the uncomfortable bed before even opening her eyes all the way. 'I'm up, I'm up.'

'I bleeped you four times, Cassie,' she hissed.

'Sorry,' Cassie said, trying in vain to fix her hair but it really wasn't any use now.

'What time did you get in?' Mary asked, a little softer.

'One,' Cassie answered as they left the small on-call room where doctors and nurses spent most of their free time sleeping.

Shutting the door behind them, her shoes clicked along with the tiled hallway floors as Cassie listened to what her job would be today.

'Aaron called out today, so you're going to be working in the radiology wing.'

Cassie looked at her surprised, 'But I haven't worked there yet.'

'That's fine, you're just going to be doing your normal job, taking vital signs and their history, you know the drill.'

Cassie nodded, even though she was a little nervous. She took the lift up to the third floor and when she stepped out she made her way to radiology and there she had seen Dylan for the first time, leaning over the reception desk, shuffling paper.

'Hello, I'm Cassie and I'll be helping you today,' she had said,

He had simply looked up at her and spoken only three words to her. 'Here, take this,' he said and unceremoniously dumped a clipboard into her hand and turned away from her.

She had blinked at him at that moment, surprised at how rude he had been, but she knew how crazy this department could get, so she had taken it and grabbed the nursing cart with everything she would need to double-check vitals before the patient could go in to have their X-Ray.

As soon as she got set up her first patient came in, she took their blood pressure, temperature, and asked how they felt and their pain level from one to ten. Of course, most of them had broken bones so they didn't feel all that well.

But even still she helped them to the X-Ray room before Dylan came in and took over from her and she would be left to go to the next patient. It went on like that for over four more hours before she finally clocked off.

Cassie made her way to the hospital cafeteria. She had almost gone back to sleep but her empty stomach had pulled her towards the smell of coffee and food.

As she walked around the room that buzzed with doctors, nurses and patients alike, she grabbed her black cup of coffee and bacon sandwich. Not the best thing in the world for her to eat but there was a reason she wasn't a dietitian.

Cassie made her way almost zombie-like to a table, the smell of bitter coffee filling her nose, mingling with the greasy and salt of the bacon. The smell had her so hypnotized as she sat down that Cassie didn't even notice the chair on the opposite side of the table being dragged out and someone sitting in it until they spoke.

'Hey.'

She jumped a little and looked up from her drink with wide eyes to see that Dylan was sitting across from her with his own drink in hand; from the grass-like smell of it she could tell it was green tea.

'Other people's bacon sandwiches always smell so

good. Nothing quite like one for breakfast.'

'To be fair, I didn't know it was breakfast time,' Cassie said and looked at the clock on her phone to see it was seven in the morning.

'How long have you been here?' he asked her as he took a drink from his cup.

'Since one last night,' Cassie answered before she took a long, long drink of her coffee, and as she did so, she watched him, his nose wrinkled up in disgust.

'What's wrong?' she asked him not so kindly. Cassie watched his green eyes go wide, maybe realizing she had seen his look.

'I... I just don't like the smell of coffee is all.'

Cassie felt her mouth open in pure shock, she had never heard of someone disliking coffee before.

'What kind of NHS worker doesn't drink coffee?' she asked, truly wanting to know.

'Coffee has always been too bitter for me,' he answered honestly.

She could only blink at him a moment at the pure insanity of it. Someone who worked in this field and didn't drink coffee, even for just the caffeine of it. No this wouldn't do, she needed to put the world back in order. She got up from her seat and made her way back to the coffee pots.

'Where are you going?' Dylan called after her, but she only grabbed a mug and started pouring.

First was the coffee; she poured the dark liquid halfway up before she turned to the creamer and poured a few tablespoons in. Then sugar and to fill the rest of the cup up Cassie topped it off with milk. It now looked nothing like the coffee she would enjoy but that was the point.

She caught the eye of the woman behind the till and gestured she would pay in a minute, then came back over to him and placed the mug down in front of him before she sat back down and took a bite of her cooling sandwich.

'Well, what are you waiting for?' Cassie asked him as he just looked down at the drink.

'What's in it?' He asked, picking it up to look at it like it held some kind of secrets.

'Drink it and find out, but I can promise it won't kill you,' Cassie answered and took a sip out of her own cup.

He eventually gave a warm smile, then, 'Fine.' He took a sip and seemed to think it over a moment before he looked at her with a raised eyebrow. 'I'm not so sure you were telling the truth about it not killing me with the amount of sugar you put in here.'

'Well, you kinda deserve it,' Cassie said, 'After how you treated me today.'

His lips slightly curved down, 'What do you mean?'

'The whole "Here take this" and then not another word from you isn't really how this works,' Cassie said, 'We're all supposed to talk and work as a team.'

He looked down at his cup a long second before he met her eyes, 'You're right; I should have been better to you. Things… things have been hard lately.'

She frowned at him, 'What do you mean?'

A couple of silent seconds passed before he muttered, 'It's something personal I can't talk about at work.'

'Well, why don't we wait until we're off the clock?' Cassie said, pushing her chair back and standing up.

Dylan looked up at her, 'What are you talking about?'

'When we finish our shift, we're off the clock we can talk about whatever we want as we walk home.'

'I guess you're right,' Dylan said as he got up and joined her, a look of curiosity clear in his eyes as to what she was doing. 'See you when we're done. Whenever that is.'

The day flew by in a haze of broken limbs and worse and Dylan went and changed out of his scrubs before Cassie joined him and they started their walk down the street, it was only a thirty-minute walk to her place anyway and the early spring night was warm in just the right way, with only a breeze here and there off the river to let them know winter was still around.

'So what did you want to say that you couldn't at work?' Cassie asked him.

He closed his eyes and let out a deep breath, 'You know I shouldn't have even said anything, I really shouldn't be pulling you into my life's problems.'

'You're not pulling me into anything, I'm the one who wants to know, that's if you're willing to tell me.'

'Fine, but please don't tell anyone else because honestly, I shouldn't even be telling you, it's not something I do with people I just meet.'

'Do you want me to cross my heart and hope to die?' Cassie asked sarcastically.

She saw him smirk a little, shaking his head before he went on, 'I'm getting a divorce from my wife and she's making it a living hell; she wants everything from me and isn't willing to move an inch on anything.'

Cassie nodded in understanding; she had never been married but she herself had messy breakups before. 'That's pretty bad; are there kids involved?

'Oh, God, no, she didn't want kids and I thank the stars for it because they would just make everything so much worse.'

'That's something at least,' Cassie said, 'Do you have anyone else you can talk to about all of this?'

He was quiet a moment before he spoke. 'No, not really, it's just me and my parents and I moved to London after I got married and left them in Cornwall.'

'So you have no one to go out with and have a drink and just rant to?' Cassie asked him, looking up and into his eyes.

Dylan laughed a little at her words, 'No, I don't go out drinking much anyway.'

'Wow, you're a radiographer who doesn't drink coffee and a man getting divorced who doesn't drink alcohol,' Cassie said with a smile.

'I know; I'm a real medical mystery,' Dylan said, smiling at himself.

'What about friends?' Cassie asked as they crossed the street.

'I'm not one to make friends easily,' Dylan answered.

'Well, now you do,' Cassie said looking up at him.

'What are you talking about?' He asked, looking at her, his green eyes flashing in the dim lights as cars passed them by.

'You have a friend to go out drinking with now,' she said and a moment later she stopped in front of a pub.

He looked up and saw the name of the building above them – The Whistler.

'Well, what are you waiting for, let's go in,' Cassie said and pushed him inside the busy room.

They made their way over to the bar where she sat down with him next to her.

She watched as he looked around himself in the packed pub. People of all kinds milled around drinking and talking to one another, the noise deafening.

'What can I get you two?' the bartender asked them as he walked over to them as he cleaned the bar top.

'Two shots of whisky please,' Cassie answered, the man nodded and stepped away from them for only a moment before two short glasses were placed in front of them.

'Bottoms up,' she said, pushing one over to him, picking up her own.

He picked the glass and looked down at the amber-coloured liquid before he drank it in one go.

She smiled and did the same. 'Another one,' Cassie said, pushing her glass over to the bartender where he poured them two more shots and, without thinking about the headache they would have in the morning, they drank them too and then another.

After twenty minutes they both sat back and Cassie knew they were both buzzed.

She looked over at Dylan who was playing with his glass but stopped when he noticed her eyes on him.

'Having fun?' Cassie asked him.

'Well, I know I won't be saying this in the morning but surprisingly I am, I haven't been to a pub since I was at uni.'

'Sounds like you really needed this then,' Cassie said.

Silence fell around them for a moment, even in the full bar but at that moment it felt like it was only them there, the music that played seemed to be muted as their eyes met.

Cassie watched as Dylan wetted his dry lips a moment before he spoke. 'You know, I have no idea who you are,

Cassie, you're just some woman I sat down with and I don't know why. I don't understand why you're doing this, why are you helping some random person you met for the first time today.'

Cassie smiled as she let out a breath before she answered him, 'I... I don't know why either. You just seemed like someone who needed to talk, and I thought maybe I walked into your department for a reason today.'

'Really?' he said, surprised, 'Maybe you were right, maybe we ran into one another for a reason.'

'Maybe,' Cassie said looking down but a moment later she looked up as Dylan pushed a piece of her blonde hair out of her face, he was so close to her, close enough that she could smell the whisky on his breath and saw just how dark green his eyes were.

Suddenly their lips met in a kiss. She pulled away a little a moment to wonder just what she was doing before they kissed again, this time it was deeper and she felt heat rise within her as Dylan pulled her closer. They stayed that way for what felt like it could have been hours.

Without saying a word, they both got up and made their way outside and the next thing Cassie knew she was in Dylan's flat. As soon as they got through the door, she dropped her bag and he let his keys fall from his fingertips to land on the coffee table before their hands were on one another once again as the door closed.

Somehow they made it to his bedroom and fell into his bed. They met in another kiss once again, his lips soft against her own. She pulled away and as he watched her, she slowly pulled off her t-shirt and let it fall to the floor. Everything about that day and night had happened by chance. Aaron calling in sick, her working with him, even the pub they stopped at. Did it all happen by chance?

Today

Cassie bit her lip hard to make herself come back to reality and to make herself stop reliving that night; she needed to focus on work – after all, people needed her to be on her best game.

Her first patient was a male teenager who was one of the people who had been in the pile-up from this morning. He had only needed four stitches above his right eyebrow. After giving him some painkillers, she moved on to her next one.

This one was a middle-aged woman who had been hurt far worse than the teen, with cuts all over her face and her neck already in a brace. 'Hello, Mrs. Berry I'm going to be your nurse today,' Cassie said as she started to take her blood pressure.

The woman said nothing to her, only looked out the window the whole time.

'Are you in pain?' Cassie asked and again she didn't get an answer and she had a feeling she wouldn't be getting much information from her; after all she was probably in shock still. 'Is there anyone I can call for you?'

Cassie wasn't surprised when she didn't answer her once again, so she turned away and towards the computer to start looking up the woman's emergency contract when she felt the soft touch of someone grabbing her arm.

'Do you know how my daughter is?' the woman asked, looking at her with watery grey eyes, 'She was in the car with me and they took her away when we got here and I don't know where she is.'

'I'm sorry; I need to take care of you first, but I can promise she's in good hands here,' Cassie said as she started to grab some butterfly plasters and alcohol wipes to start cleaning her face but Mrs. Berry pulled away from her.

'Find my daughter, please.'

'Let me help you first and then I'll go and look –'

'No, I'll do whatever you want after you tell me where my Anna is.'

Cassie closed her eyes a moment knowing she would do what the woman had asked before she opened them back up and nodded. 'I'll go and see where she is and then I'll be back.'

She opened the curtains that divided the beds and closed them as she made her way to the nursing station.

Alice looked up at her from where she had been typing away at the keyboard, 'Hey what's up?'

'Do you know if there was a person with the name of Anna Berry being admitted?' Cassie asked.

'Give me one minute,' Alice said as she clicked around with the mouse a second before she started typing once again.

It only took her a few minutes for her to pull up the name. 'She's going to surgery as soon as there's a slot, for a broken leg.'

'Who was her doctor?' Cassie asked, wanting as much information as she could get to put Mrs. Berry at ease.

'Umm, it was Doctor Williams.'

'Okay, and where is she now?'

'She's getting another X-Ray to see precisely what needs to be done when there is a theatre free. She ... let me see, she has an open fracture. Looks nasty.'

'Who's the radiographer?' Cassie asked looking back at the curtains.

'You already know the answer,' Alice said, giving her a knowing look.

Cassie let out a breath as she looked up at the ceiling, the yellow lights shining down on them, far from the sunny day outside.

'You're going to go up and see how the girl is doing, aren't you?' Alice asked.

'You know me far too well,' Cassie said as she turned away from her friend and started for the lift but she still heard Alice mutter something under her breath, 'I know the both of you too well.'

Cassie pressed the button and the doors slid open and she stepped into the silver walled box. It was a long, long minute that she had to stand there with the mindlessly happy music playing. Finally, a ding rang out and she stepped into the all too familiar hallway.

Cassie watched for the red light over the door which warned not to go in without a lead apron and when it had flashed and gone out, she slipped into the room where she saw Dylan and another nurse talking.

A moment later Dylan looked up as if he could sense

she was there and their eyes met before Cassie looked back down. Dylan checked the screen to make sure the views were okay and nodded at the nurse, who went round from behind the screen and wheeled out Anna Berry, dosed up on pain-killers but looking by and large okay. Cassie waited until the nurse had gone before either one of them spoke.

'What are you doing up here?' Dylan asked, turning to look at her.

'Honestly I came up here for Mrs. Berry. She wanted to know where her daughter was and if she was doing okay.'

'You can come in to see the X-Rays yourself,' Dylan said, stepping aside to let her behind the lead glass screen.

Cassie knew she shouldn't but moved round in front of the screen anyway, the whole time telling herself this was to make Mrs. Berry feel better. Dylan stepped closer and dimmed the lights a little.

She stood back as he went over to the computer and pulled up the X-Ray that had already been sent to the surgeon. Cassie could see where the break had been, the tibia had broken cleanly, but it had moved out of place and there would need to be at least a couple of pins inserted to keep the bone in place for the healing process.

'Thank you, her mother will feel better, I'm sure, knowing it's just a broken bone,' Cassie said and was just about to turn away but stopped as a hand gently grabbed her wrist.

Cassie paused, her eyes closing a second before she slowly turned back to Dylan.

'Cassie –' he started but she stopped him with her own words.

'Please don't do this, not here,' Cassie begged, she didn't want to be a subject of gossip unless this was for real.

'All I want to say is that I hate that our day was ruined, I wanted that coffee with you, I wanted that day to have with just you.'

Cassie met his eyes and saw the truth in them, the heat in them, before she had to look away. 'I did too, I wanted to be with you and not worry about people seeing us, not worry about getting in trouble, just be with you like... like a real couple,' Cassie said letting herself get closer to him at that moment.

'Is that what you want?' Dylan asked her, 'You want us to be together in a relationship?'

'Of course I do,' Cassie answered. It's all I've wanted for so long, she didn't say.

Dylan looked down at her for a long moment before he pulled her closer to him suddenly and their lips met in a kiss. Cassie let herself melt into his embrace, her hands finding their way to his hair, her fingers tangled into his brown curls. She could taste the green tea he loved so dearly on his lips.

He started moving down then, to the soft skin of her neck, sucking at her collarbone and she knew that in the morning there would be a small purple mark she would make sure to cover up... or maybe she wouldn't, maybe she would let everyone see and when someone asked her who had done it, she would tell them.

Suddenly a sound made both of them jump back from one another. Cassie hurriedly stepped back just in time for the nurse from before to walk into the room.

She looked at both of them a moment, maybe wondering why Cassie was still there.

'Thank you for showing me the X-Ray, her mother will feel a lot better,' Cassie said as she quickly made her way over to the door and opened it but she stopped and looked back where she found his eyes still on her.

Cassie let the ghost of a smile played on her lips as she turned away and closed the door behind herself. Minutes later she passed by Alice's desk. Cassie caught her eyes and saw the little look the other woman shot at her, as if she knew what they had done.

Cassie felt her cheeks heat a little as she passed her, but she made sure to look professional as she stepped through the curtains where she found Mrs. Berry still sitting in the A&E bed looking out of the window at the summer sun. Cassie quickly informed the older women of how her daughter was and she saw her relax and, finally, she was able to treat her cuts and check her vitals.

Afterwards, she stepped out from the curtains and was just about to make her way over to her next patient when she heard the sound of her phone buzzing at her to answer it. Cassie quickly made her way to the bathroom and locked herself in one of the stalls before she opened the message. Carrying personal phones at work was strictly forbidden, but everyone did it – being called in from a day off meant being cut some slack, surely?

'Hey I didn't get to finish what I was saying to you and I can't just write it in a text. So after work let's meet up at The Whistler, 10:30.'

Cassie smiled to herself as she read 'The Whistler'. The pub she had taken him by mere chance, she herself had never been there before that night but now it was special to her even if it was just a pub.
She sent a quick text back. 'Race you there.'

The rest of the day seemed to go by in a blur for Cassie. She saw patient after patient, going about her work on cloud nine, her smile never seeming to fall. Finally, the clock hit nine and Cassie made her way to the locker room and took off her scrubs. She looked up as she heard the door open and saw Alice walking in.

'You headed home to get some sleep?' Alice asked, pulling her red shirt over her head.

'You know I'm not,' Cassie said, grabbing her bag and shutting her locker before she snapped the lock in place.

Alice turned to her with the small smile that reminded her of an all-knowing older sister. 'Where are the two of you headed?'

'The Whistler, do you know it?' Cassie answered, pulling on the black hoodie she always kept in her locker.

'That sounds like a date,' Alice said, shaking her head. She lived way out west in Wimbledon and rarely socialised in town.

'He wants to tell me something,' Cassie said a little shyly.

'Are you guys going to make it official finally?'

'I don't know, maybe,' Cassie answered, 'I guess I'll find out, won't I?'

'I guess you will,' Alice said, giving her one last smile before Cassie turned away and stepped outside. As she walked, a warm summer breeze lifted her blonde hair and blew it around her face and for a moment she let her surroundings soak in. London was so many things. A home, a tourist stop to others. But Cassie knew that she was happy here, though she wasn't sure if it was because of how breathtakingly beautiful it could be, with lights that made it shine at night, and there was so much to see or was it because of the people she knew... because she had met Dylan here.

Cassie crossed the river and dived into the small streets that she had already come to know so well and smiled to herself as she saw a woman, probably drunk, shouting at a friend, 'You're filthy! You're disgusting! You're fired!' – someone had been watching too much of *The Apprentice*!

Cassie crossed the street then, the green light catching in her hair making it alight with neon green as she stopped in front of The Whistler. She took a deep breath, the smell of ale in the air, half-smiling at the two bouncers staring at her from the door. The larger of the two pulled open the door for her. Instantly she was hit with noise. The place was packed tonight but that was fine with her; she caught sight of a young girl dressed as a princess hiding under a table staring off with a dog, poor kid, her mother should be ashamed.

She made her way to the bar where she had sat with Dylan what seemed so long ago now.

'What can I get you tonight?' The bartender asked.

'Two shots of whisky,' Cassie answered as she pulled out her phone and saw the time was 10:20. Cassie smiled to herself as she sent a text to Dylan. 'Beat you here, that means you get to pay for the next round.' She hit send before she placed her phone on the bar top as she picked up her shot and drank it in one go.

'Another one please,' Cassie said, pointing to her glass and the bartender nodded. She had a feeling she would be needing the liquid courage tonight for some reason.

Cassie turned to watch the door for Dylan. Suddenly her phone screen lit up showing the time to be 10:22 pm.

22:22

Maryanne Coleman

Working at The Whistler wasn't all bad. If she said it in her head, it sounded okay but not very convincing. Perhaps with different emphasis. Working at The Whistler wasn't *all* bad. Working at The Whistler wasn't all *bad.*

She shook her head as she wove her way between tables filled with shouting, pissed people, holding the tray above her head so that no gesticulating dickhead could knock it out of her hands. It was no good; no matter how you said it, that statement simply wasn't true. Working at The Whistler was absolutely shite. There were no tips worthy of the name – people simply didn't tip a waitress who brought a giant tray full of mini-burgers each costing a king's ransom and which tasted of nothing. They hardly noticed they had arrived, just shovelling them into their mouths, regardless. One night, one particularly awful night, she had dolloped some extra-fiery chilli sauce in one and she and the chef had huddled, giggling inside the swing door to hear the screams.

Nothing.

Not a peep. The drunken oaf who had shovelled it in hadn't even noticed.

So now, she just did what she had to do. Glasses in. Food out. Plates in. More food out.

But by ten o'clock, sanity had begun to reassert itself, just as it always did. Last orders for food was at quarter to ten and nothing took long to eat, at The Whistler. By ten, it was clearing up, mainly. The clientele remained as obnoxious as ever, right to the last drop. And with automatic extensions every night – hen parties, stag parties … she wondered again, why they weren't called cock parties … leaving do's, even the odd gender reveal – she would still be on her feet for an hour or more. But not having to look at braying arseholes spraying half chewed burger everywhere was certainly a bonus that the later hours brought, and she was learning to be grateful for small mercies.

She bum-bumped the swing door and took her latest batch of dirties through into the kitchen, where the washer-up was, as always, up to his eyebrows in suds and steam. An automatic washer was out of the question for The Whistler – the turn around needed was too short and the thickness of the jammy lipstick stains on half the glasses was too recalcitrant for any machine yet invented. She dumped the tray of glasses down and spun round the end of the prep counter to go out of the other door. No one spoke. By ten o'clock, they were all tired beyond words.

The chef was cleaning down. He always got a slightly smug look on his face around about now. If he played his cards right, he could be out of the door by ten fifteen. He could read a crowd better than Derren Brown. He could tell from the level of noise from about eight whether they were eaters or drinkers and it was a rare night when he got it wrong. Tonight, they had been mainly drinkers. A stag do dressed as Power Rangers had taken one look at the prices and buggered off for kebabs down the street. The hedge-funders had had a bad day and were looking to be legless by ten – as the door swung open, she could see they had succeeded. A tray of glasses hit the deck followed by scattered applause and some cat calls. Without even thinking, she swung back round through the 'in' door to get a broom and dustpan.

In the kitchen, something had changed. Something about the atmosphere made her hair stand up on the back of her neck. The chef was standing at bay against the hob and a man she didn't know was in the doorway, his eyes bulging and his finger raised, pointing, trembling, at him.

'And,' he said, scarcely noticing that someone else had come in, 'if you touch my wife again, I'll …' he looked around wildly and lunged at the knife rack, pulling one out at random, 'I'll cut your nuts off for you. Then see how you manage around decent women.'

He threw the knife on the floor and stormed out, leaving a stunned silence in his wake. The washer-up turned back to his suds, but he couldn't suppress a smile. The smug bastard, lording it over them all because he had City and Guilds in catering, basic. He hoped he did have his nuts cut off; that would cramp his style.

She turned to the chef for explanation, but he shrugged at her and ripped off his apron, then stormed out as well. Her heart sank a little, but not much. Sometimes, when it hadn't been too busy and she could still feel her feet, she would go round to his for a quickie, but it wasn't as if her heart were broken. Even so … she just hoped no one knew. She didn't want to look a fool.

And so, back she went, for another tray of glasses. The taps roared their water into the sink. The trays clashed, the plates slid and slithered.

In all the clash and carry, no one heard the hiss. No one heard the gas escaping where the chef, in his confusion and hurry, had turned the knob just far enough to turn the jets on, not far enough for them to ignite. The gas crept into the kitchen, replacing the air insidiously and no one knew …

The washer-up looked up with his hangdog eyes, ready for

another tray of glasses as the door swung open. But it wasn't glasses. It was the manager.

He looked around him, in the supercilious way that got up everyone's nose.

'Where's that bloody chef?' he asked.

The washer-up shrugged. 'Gone.'

'Gone? Why's he bloody gone? It's only just gone quarter past ten.'

'No more food orders,' the washer-up said, 'no more chef.'

The manager waved a piece of paper. 'I've got an order, here,' he snapped. He didn't add that he had taken it himself without looking at the time. There were lots of rules in The Whistler, but the most inviolate was 'Thou shalt not make the manager look a dick.'

The washer-up shrugged again and wiped a soapy hand across his forehead. 'He's gone, though.' Perhaps the chef would get the sack. Perhaps he, trained by his own dear Mama in her kitchen back in Sicily, would step up. Perhaps … he sighed as he dreamed his soapy dream.

The manager stood there, chewing his lip in fury. There was nothing else for it. He would have to do it himself. He reached for the apron and tied it round his waist. It was only halloumi and salad, not exactly rocket science. He snatched a block of it from the fridge and savagely cut it into slices. He lined them up on the grill pan, looking again at the order – five portions. He looked at what he had laid out. Bugger. Six. Wastage. Never mind – they would do a good Tripadvisor if they got more than they expected. He saw the time on the order – oh, double bugger; he had already been too long. He looked up at the clock and swore under his breath. Just gone twenty past ten. Bugger, bugger, bugger. He grated black pepper over the halloumi and made the washer-up wince. The door swung open and the waitress came in with another load of glasses.

He reached up to the grill and slid the pan under, coughing a little as he reached up.

'Is it me, or is the air a bit thick in here?' He coughed again. 'Sorry. Frog in my throat.'

He pressed the button to ignite the grill.

* * *

Somehow, the silence inside The Whistler seemed all the more profound because of the chaos outside. Every now and then, a beam creaked or a lump of plaster fell from a wall. Here and there, the last air left a chest which had ceased to harbour life at 10.22 precisely. Bursts of static made the giant TV mounted on the wall in the corner flash and quiver. Then, suddenly, with savage clarity, a generic newsreader, the kind they put on late at night when only the insomniac and the desperate are awake, appeared, with a piece missing across the top of her head where the screen had splintered.

'News is just in that an explosion has ripped through The Whistler pub in London's bustling area of Soho,' she solemnly announced, her face giving away nothing, as she had been taught. 'Eye-witnesses report it took place at 22:22. First responders are on scene. The number of casualties within The Whistler is not clear at present and it is unknown if this was an act of terrorism or a tragic accident, though the loss of life is, sadly, expected to be high.'

She paused, looking solemn. She hadn't many expressions, but solemn was one she did well.

'We'll bring you more on that story as it comes in.' With practised ease she rearranged her face and then continued, 'Brighton stunned fans tonight by beating Chelsea 2-1 away...'

THE
WHISTLER

Other titles by the authors for your consideration:

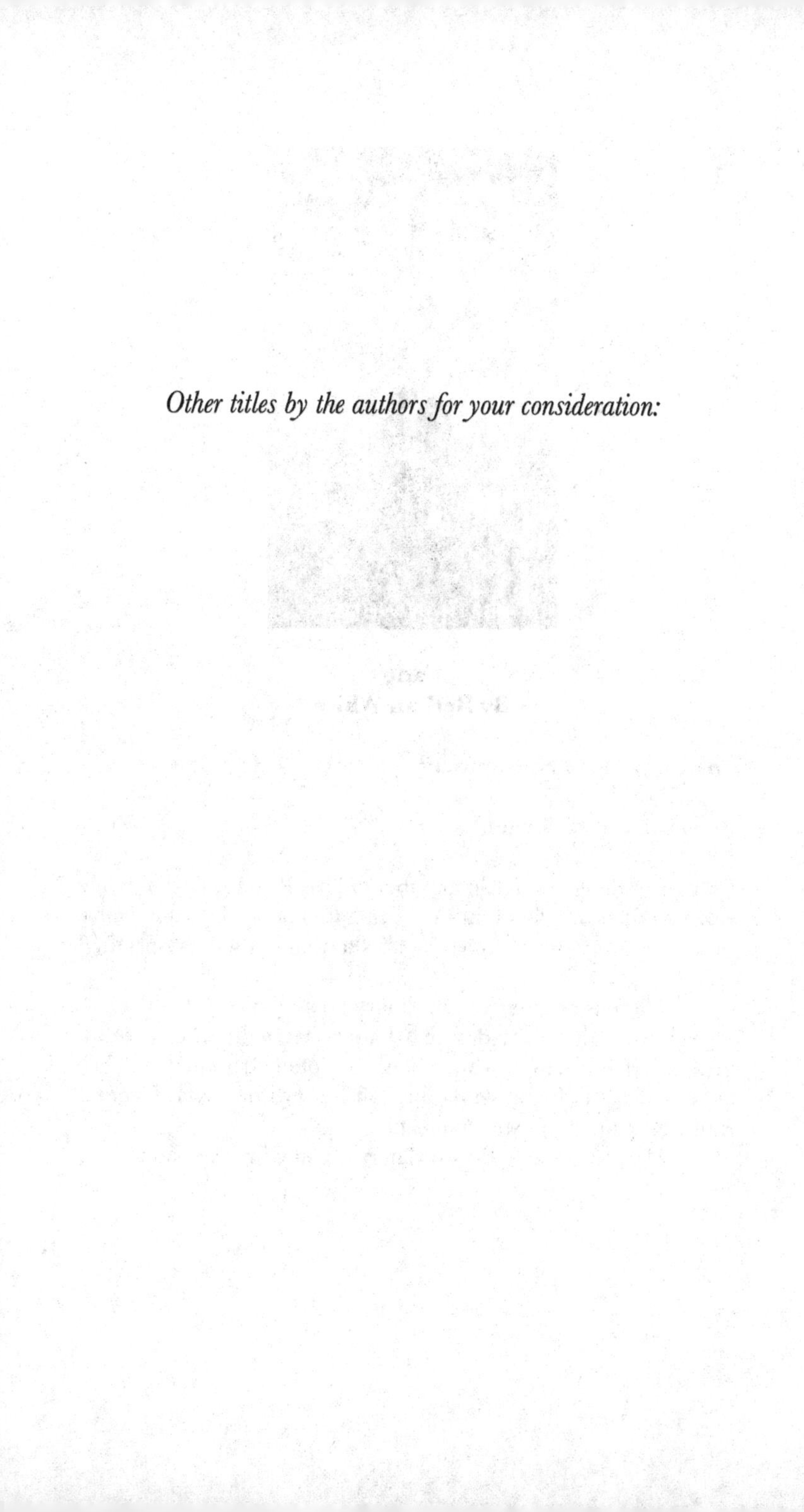

Fade
By Bethan White

Do you want to remember?

Do you want to forget?

There is nothing extraordinary about Chris Rowan. Each day he wakes to the same faces, has the same breakfast, the same commute, the same sort of homes he tries to rent out to unsuspecting tenants.

There is nothing extraordinary about Chris Rowan. That is apart from the black dog that haunts his nightmares and an unexpected encounter with a long forgotten demon from his past. A nudge that will send Chris on his own downward spiral, from which there may be no escape.

There is nothing extraordinary about Chris Rowan...

Daisy Chains
By Samantha Evergreen

After a wild night of partying on the last day of spring break, three seventeen-year-old friends Rose, Lily, and Violet wake up to find their best friend Daisy Young is missing and in the small town of Watkinsville, Georgia in 1975 that's not normal.

As the days go by, everyone starts to wonder how the girl who spent her days with her head in the clouds and had no enemies could go missing. Rumours start that she ran away; that's until Rose, Lily, and Violet find bones in a riverbank.

Watkinsville descends into madness as Chief Thompson and the newly instated 21-year-old Officer Mark Hollow look into what had happened that night. But only more questions arise as men from around town start to confess for no reason, all with the same story. So Rose, Lily, and Violet and Officer Hollow take it upon themselves to find the killer.

But little do they know they're running against the clock and things may not be quite what they seem.

**The Vulture King
By Nikki Turner**

Orphaned Aram has survived alone for five years, his only friend a thieving magpie, who acts as his eyes. For in the Carrionlands, magic comes at a terrible price. It costs you your sight, hearing or voice.

When he rescues a voiceless girl, Bina, from being sacrificed to the Vulture King, he is taken in by an underground resistance group. They reveal that Aram's mother is alive, but the king is using her and other slave magicians to fuel his unnaturally long life.

With his mother's magic being rapidly drained, she doesn't have long to live. If Aram can find the Radix, a hidden magical power source, there's a slim chance he might be able to save her. But to get there, he must cross the Barrens where every living creature is out to kill you. That's if one of his new companions doesn't betray him first.

A Storm of Magic
By Ashley Laino

Being brought back from the dead is an impressive trick, even for magician Darien Burron. Now he must try and use his sleight of hand to swindle modern-day witch, Mirah, to sign her power away, or end up a tormented demon in the afterlife.

Meanwhile, sixteen-year-old Mirah is starting to lose control of her powers. After an incident at her aunt's Witchery store, Mirah is sent to a secret coven to learn to control her abilities. While away, Mirah meets up with a soft-spoken clairvoyant, a brazen storm witch, and the creator of dark magic itself. The young woman must learn to trust in herself before she loses herself entirely to the darkness that hunts her.

Soft Hunger
By Lucrezia Brambillaschi

Soft Hunger is a beautiful collection of poetry that treads the delicate line between intimate and public, between talking to oneself and talking to a crowd.

Pain, loss, heartbreak, depression and, above all else, always, the crowning glory of existence: love - these are the core themes you will find in this collection. But also the struggle of being part of a so-called minority, the pride in finally finding and being comfortable with one's own identity, the compelling need to change the world and the audacity to try and do that through words.

Through a continuous movement between the inside and the outside, the soft-spoken and the screamed, the obvious and the implied, this collection of poetry takes the reader into the intricacies of feelings, offering raw honesty, brutal emotion and the reassurance that no one is alone, we're all human after all.

No Faff, No Fuss, Just Food
By Maryanne Coleman

No Fuss, No Faff, Just Food is a cookery book for people who have better things to do than slave over a hot stove. Filled with suggestions as well as recipes and thoughtfully peppered with pages for your own ideas, this book takes the lid off the simmering worries which many people have when cooking for themselves, family and friends – cooking should be fun, not scary, and reading this romp through possibly the most relaxed kitchen in the world will have you laughing as well as, very soon, cooking like you mean it!

Recipes in *No Fuss, No Faff, Just Food* include main meals, snacks, basic techniques and – of course – chocolate cake! There's no point in a recipe book with no chocolate cake in it and as a bonus, it is gluten and dairy free! Safety in the kitchen, from sharp knives to anaphylactic shock, avoidance of, is covered as well as some yummy recipes.

If you only ever have one cookery book, make it this one.

BLKDOG

www.blkdogpublishing.com